ALL MEN ARE CASUALTIES

BOOK 2 IN THE 'GLIDERS OVER NORMANDY' SERIES

THOMAS WOOD

Visit my website at www.ThomasWoodBooks.com

Printed in the United Kingdom

First Printing: September 2018
by
BoleynBennett Publishing

For my wife, Rachael, for her unwavering support and belief in me.

*"The Hun believes that only a fool will go to Normandy.
That is why I am going!"*

—General Richard 'Windy' Gale
Commanding Officer 6th Airborne Division

GRAB ANOTHER BOOK FOR FREE

PART I

1

6th June 1944
00.16 hours

MY HEAD POUNDED, and my spine felt as if it was being stretched as I began to come round. I arched my back in earnest trying to realign my body and subdue some of the pain.

My chin was tucked into my chest and my arms felt heavy as they drooped limply down by my sides. A dull ache emanated from them as blood was reintroduced, a pulsating feeling as it was pumped round my limbs.

Everything seemed in total darkness.

My eyes were heavy as I tried desperately to take in as much information as I could. My cockpit was ruined, the windscreen had vanished, my controls had been eaten up by a mixture of bushes and barbed wire, and my seat creaked as it clung precariously to the main body of the aircraft.

I sucked in a mouthful of air sharply, as I tried to regain my normal levels of consciousness. Slowly, reluctantly, I began to lift my head. It was heavy with the added weight of a helmet and as I undid the straps, letting it fall into my lap, a large dent was clearly visible in the centre, where I had collided with the solid structure around me.

The darkness was captivating and it took me a few seconds of adjustment before I could begin to make out the outlines of objects around me.

Warm liquid began to run over my left eye and as I wiped it away discovered that I had a small crater in my head, just on the hairline, that was flowing down slowly like an obstructed waterfall. I plugged the gap momentarily with my index finger, in the same way that a leaky pipe, spurting water everywhere would be stemmed.

Brushing my hair over the wound, I pushed a clump into the hole, feeling it soak up the moisture almost immediately. I let it cling to my head, allowing it to stop the flow of blood from dripping down into my eyes.

My ears had popped, and I tried to clear them desperately by pinching my nose hard and blowing violently, putting so much pressure on my brain that it felt as if it would burst from my skull. Nothing worked, I was temporarily deaf.

My neck creaked and cracked as I commanded enough energy to lift my weary head and look around me. I allowed myself a quick roll of my skull, my vertebrae popping with each degree that I rotated.

As I looked over to my left, it took a moment or two for me to realise what I was seeing. I felt my eyes narrow and expand as my brain struggled to register the simplest information. The seat where my pilot, Charlie Manning, should be sat, was no longer there. The wooden floor where his chair should have been firmly housed, was completely bare, except for a series of large gouges running along towards the controls.

Desperate to not let the invasion begin without me, I began unbuckling myself, yanking and snatching at the clutches of the Horsa. She had been a faithful craft up till this point but now I had a different job to do, she would have to let me go.

My ears slowly began to tune back in to the environment I was in and I stopped as I tried to make out an unusual noise. My jaw hung open and my breathing ceased as I willed whatever it was to echo again.

A low rumble was coming from straight in front of me, I couldn't tell what it was. I cocked my head to one side, so the noise could hit my ear more directly, hoping earnestly that I would be able to decipher the moan from in front of me. As the midnight breeze drifted over the field, a low, constant hiss carried more audible sounds to my awaiting ear.

The groan intensified from a quiet breathing to a more determined grunt. Silence ensued.

Then, a cough.

"Johnny."

I still couldn't get my head around it, a few moments after, a plea rasped out once more.

"Johnny, get me out of here," he was Home Counties, not quite a Rupert, but not your East End Cockney that I had been blessed with. It was an accent that I had never experienced until I met him, it was an accent of some far away society, reserved only for royalty or the newsreader on the wireless.

The silence that engulfed his speech was haunting. I heard no shuffles, no swaying of bushes or snapping of twigs. Not even any gunshots. Just total, deathly silence.

"Come on John, you there, mate?"

"Yeah, I'm here, give me a minute."

I wasn't entirely sure if my reassurance was as convincing as I'd hoped. Fiddling around in my breast pocket, I found the small torch that I had for navigation, it was a funny looking thing, given to me by an American back at base in exchange for a taste of some corned beef, I'd come away from that particular transaction feeling very proud of myself.

The torch was heavy, in a sort of L shape, and flicking the switch on the side gave a small orange glow to the surrounding area, made smaller by the tape I'd filled most of the glass with, to restrict the potential target I'd become. Its pinprick of light wavered and shook slightly as I directed it towards the noise, and I used my free hand to grip my wrist to steady myself. Shutting my eyes momentarily, I breathed heavily, trying to compose myself and let the nausea pass.

Charlie was lying face down in a bush, still strapped in faithfully to his chair. He looked like a lost little boy. His arms and legs were flailing outwards, as if he was paddling to keep himself afloat. It served no purpose here, all he was achieving was tangling himself up in weeds and scratching himself on thorns.

My head pounded almost in unison with my heart. I shut my eyes for a second and let the stinging sensation die down.

For a moment, I was back home. Watching my brother as he dangled from a tree by his arm, clinging on for his life. He screamed and hollered at me to help him, but I was too far away. He was out of my reach.

I needed to help him, he wanted me to save him, it was my job, my *duty* to stop my younger brother from coming to harm.

I stared at him, knowing with absolute certainty that he was about to be hurt. He was high up, the best he could hope for would be a broken leg, and all manner of other injuries besides.

The branch was too weak though, it was already creaking and straining under his considerably lighter load, if I was to clamber across, we would both end up falling.

He had done well to hold himself where he was, he had slipped higher up and managed to clamp himself to the branch he now clung to.

Blood dripped intermittently from the bottom of his chin. It had rolled from a wound just under his eyebrow and trickled slowly like a lake rippling in a gentle breeze. I was fixated with the droplet as it began to cling loosely to his face before leaping to the ground. That single droplet of scarlet fluid had brought me so much peace, so much tranquillity, that I began to question why it had brought so much serenity to me.

He began to cry. Even he, with his unquestioning trust in me, knew his situation was helpless. The branch began to crack and all I could do was watch as he plummeted to the ground.

"Johnny," he hissed, "you helping me or what?"

He twisted his face to the side, as the light graced his helpless being.

"Get that light off me, Johnny, I want to get home you know," he screwed his face up tightly as he spoke, not wanting to turn his face back into the pit of thorns.

I let out a small snort of laughter as I observed him squirming in the bush in his comical predicament.

"Come on, there's twigs going up me nose here!"

That only added to my glee, he'd always been the one to get lucky with everything and watch me sort my mess out, now, finally, it was the other way around.

Lobbing my helmet back on top of my throbbing skull I began to shuffle around trying to get out of the aircraft.

I couldn't move.

"Charlie," I hissed in an aggressive whisper, "I can't move, I'm caught in the wire."

The more I stared at my lower legs tangled in the barbed wire, the more the pain grew. The small, rusty spikes had penetrated my clothes and the more I wriggled, the more I felt them pierce my skin. Sweeping the flash-light's gaze away from the bush, I redirected its gaze onto my legs. Small, axe-like daggers had embedded them-selves into my shins, and hooked themselves on the under-side of my skin, threatening to rip through the other side and double the size of each fleshy puncture.

Keeping my gloves on I began the excruciating task of picking out the needles one by one, a new bead of blood rolling down my leg with every extraction. The warmth of my blood trickling down my legs felt nice in the midnight chill, almost luxurious. The adrenaline of being in charge of an aircraft gliding to the ground had begun to lose its effect, and my muscles began to cramp up with the cold. The clanging and quiet jingling of the wire as I fiddled with it, rang out across the landscape, as I psyched myself up to pull out the next piece of wire. Every minute twig of wire ripped at my trousers some more, to the point where I possessed nothing more than a piece of fraying fabric, wrapped around my legs. I let my mind wander as I thought about how long it would be before I could get my hands on a new pair. Or if I'd ever make it far enough to need some.

My leather gloves were ruined, great pockmarks of skin beamed out at me, and I could see the sweat glistening in the crevices of my palm. With a grunt of annoyance and frustration, I whipped them off and threw them impatiently to the ground.

"I'm coming, Grandad." How he came to get this nickname bemused me and everyone else he met. He was just a year or two older than me, and by far he was not the oldest on the base. I had been given credit for coming up with this endearing name and yet, I could not pinpoint the moment I had supposedly conjured it up. It was probably one of the many times that I had lost hours of my recollection to the disgusting liquid the Americans classed as Whiskey.

"About time, Boy."

I twisted myself round and gripping the top of the doorway that separated us from the troops, heaved myself feet first through the gap.

They all looked as if they'd been sent into a sleep by a deranged hypnotist. The men sat, legs up on the bench in front of them, heads down into their chest, fast asleep. Their weapons lay ready on their legs, some even with fingers on triggers in anticipation. I could see no faces, just the mesh on top of helmets, a sea of khaki, with no hint of skin, no sign of life.

Only an hour before they had been jovially singing and bantering with each other, smoking and exchanging stories. Their eyes had told a different story; the upbeat exterior was merely a façade, one that they kept up as each of them fought their own battles as they flew towards death.

Everything was still hauntingly silent. I'd have to come back to them in a minute.

I grabbed my Sten, the cold steel of which was instantly comparable with the midnight air which battered my face, and, as I hopped out, my legs gave way under the excruciating pain, my body landing un-majestically with a solid thump.

The midnight dew began to permeate my skin, refreshing my face and removing from its surface the oily remnants of perspiration. I lay there for a moment, drinking in my surroundings, listening for any sudden changes. I had never experienced silence before. I thought I had, quite often, but lying there I realised what a cacophony of noise I had heard instead of silence. My heart banged like a drum against the inside of my mind, and only in between each pumping motion, did I experience true silence. It was totally barren. My mind wandered as I lay with my eyes closed, and I felt like if I was to reopen them, I should see a totally blank canvas, nothing, just pure, brilliant white. A totally desolate landscape to accompany the neglection of noise.

With a growing agitation, I realised that my previous experience of silence was preferable to the one that I now found myself in. The hatred that I discovered for silence grew as the feeling of an impending doom took a tight grip on me, especially when I was convinced of the barrage of noise that was just moments away.

I had crashed to the ground with such a clatter that I half expected to give away the entire invasion force. I held my breath as I waited for jackboots to squeak across the field and for a hard-nosed German to point a revolver in my general direction.

I found myself hoping that I would never see the bullet exit the revolver, and that I wouldn't know what was going on. I forced my eyelids up, but they wouldn't budge. Maybe the bullet had already come. The silence that I had never before experienced brought with it a peace that I had never encountered before either. This, I thought, was death.

But everything remained perfectly still, a serene silence clinging to the French countryside. The only movement was me. The only noise from my own breathing.

I felt like the only living being among the dead.

I was a ghost.

2

6th June 1944
00.17 hours

I TRIED my best to stifle a laugh as I arrived around the front of the aircraft.

It would have been comical if I had been greeted with a nicer sight.

These Horsas were designated to be single-use aircraft, and it was probably just as well. It was a mess. The cockpit was held onto the rest of the craft by two small planks of wood running from the main body of the glider to the front. They had begun to splinter and had creaked as I shifted my body weight from the front to the back of the craft. It wouldn't be long before they gave way and came down on top of Charlie.

The main body of the Horsa had split in two. The long tube where the sleeping soldiers were, had separated cleanly from the tail of the aircraft, which lay solemnly about 100 yards away from the rest of the crash site.

A cloud must have parted, allowing the silvery sparkle of the moonlight to glare down on us, like a flare, making everything around us visible to the human eye. I waited for the inevitable crack of gunfire. I could see the other gliders now, not too far from where I was standing. I'd known that they must have been there, but the silence that emanated from them too, made them invisible to me.

I leant back for a moment, trying to sneak a glimpse at the bridge, our target. I knew it was there, I had seen it briefly as we had come down, somewhere over the other side of the glider, standing there in the darkness. I prayed there on the spot that I would live long enough to get across it.

Charlie's chair was still face down in the bush and as I kept my laughter subdued I observed the wreckage before me.

Charlie was lying with his face in the bush, his seat threatening to push him down further under the weight. The only thing that was keeping him floating on top of the foliage was the snake pit of barbed wire that slithered its way around him.

"Grandad, I'm going to need you to stay nice and still while I do this okay?"

"Why, what you thinking?"

He didn't want to know what I was thinking. My brain throbbed more intensely as I was overcome with guilt, impatience and defeat. I screwed my eyes tight, trying to block my surroundings out.

I didn't want this. I didn't want to be here.

He would have wanted me to be thinking through a

resolution to his predicament, listening to me foraging around for wire cutters before slowly snapping away at the spiralling metal that clung to his body.

The truth was, he was not even going through my mind right now, he was barely on the periphery. I felt like plonking myself down on the dampened grass, like a worn-out toddler, in a moment of contemplation.

Thoughts of my father engulfed my mind, strangling me almost, with a crippling fear of what might lay ahead of me. He had warned me, like so many others, when they had first left for training.

Charlie had been told that he would put his own survival above anyone else's even if he had the intentions of helping his friends. I considered that thought now. I was in the middle of a field in a foreign country, a country where twenty odd years ago my own father had been fighting. Charlie was my mate, my best mate, at least I thought he was. We only spoke to one another when we were picked for the same glider, me as his co-pilot. He had excelled in his flight training and so was instantly given the title of pilot with me as his sidekick. We had bonded well but I wondered whether or not I would have been given the same level of attention had I not been locked in close proximity with him on a daily basis.

Charlie was naturally a self-confessed introvert, forced out of his shell by his natural capability as a glider pilot. He frequently locked himself in his own mind, quite content with his own thoughts and on more than one occasion I was convinced that new and completely different worlds were constructed in that head of his. Worlds that no one else was allowed to see. We could only guess at what he was thinking and, even then, we'd probably be miles off.

An element of doubt began creeping into my mind. Why had he stuck with me? Maybe it was out of a sense of duty, and to make things less awkward for himself. Maybe he felt like he needed to keep an eye on me, making sure I was always ready to disconnect myself from a heavy bomber, and fall to the earth, safely. Or maybe it was a genuine friendship that we possessed.

The target was now over to my right, over the other side of our wreckage, the moon beating down upon the surrounding area. I was a sniper's dream target; lit up, motionless, vulnerable.

At the thought, I thrust myself against the body of the Horsa, as if its frail, wooden frame would offer me some sort of protection when a bullet zipped through the structure.

My breathing was laboured and loud enough to be heard from miles away. I absorbed air desperately through my nose and it faltered as I expelled it back into the night. My throat wheezed pathetically as I struggled to maintain a decent level of oxygen in my lungs.

With every breath, I made so much noise I may as well have been launching pots and pans at the bridge, singing the national anthem.

Charlie could hear my wavering breathing.

"Johnny, come on," he violently rasped.

Water streamed down from my eyes as I fought with my own mind to help my best friend, I was failing myself, but more importantly right now, I was failing him. This isn't what he had wanted, he wanted someone who he could rely on, someone he could trust. He'd made that perfectly clear while we were training. He was a fun character, always up for a laugh or a mess about, but he always had a painfully serious side, always stopping short of taking it too far, something I regularly failed in. Maybe that's where 'Grandad' had come from.

My strenuous breaths were interrupted by a desperate plea.

"Please mate," he uttered calmly, a tone of complete resignation in his voice. It pierced my soul. The sound of a man begging to be helped is something that I would never forget. I didn't like it when he spoke like that, he had the air of a severely disappointed parent, the kind of tone when a young child lets down their parent in front of the local vicar, by announcing how he had learnt his new swear word at the age of seven. Thirteen years had passed by now and my mum still went scarlet red at the very mention of that anecdote.

I rubbed my sweating palms over my face as I tried in earnest to pull myself together, I was letting my mind wander, something I knew I shouldn't do, it would get me killed. I was panicking, and I wasn't even in action yet. I began to let my sweat soaked hands slide down my oily face.

The vision that flashed across my eyes as I closed them, forced them wide open again immediately.

Even when I was a young boy, I knew that my dad was different to the way he should have been born, but it wasn't until I was older that I came to learn what it was that made him different. I had never known my father with normal skin, in fact I had only ever seen it once or twice.

The skin around my father's back looked tender and fragile, like a thin piece of paper stretched out after being tightly scrunched into a ball. I was mesmerised by the incredible craters that flooded his back, like a landscape of rolling hills, that unevenly bumped their way from top to bottom. The redness of his skin also surprised me. It had been years since it had happened but always looked just as raw as if it had happened ten minutes ago.

His pain, like the redness, never seemed to subside over time either. The grunts and grimaces that were felt around the house as ointment was massaged into the wound was a childhood memory, more like a normality, ingrained in the mind.

We all knew it was there, so why he tried to hide it from the family was beyond me.

I gave myself a mental slapping as I let my hands rub down my face and then down my chest to rid myself of a layer of clammy perspiration.

I didn't want that for myself, I needed to be careful. But I also needed to help my best friend, he couldn't lie there forever.

Cut away. Leave it, you have a job to do. Come on.

Psyching myself up with a rapid, sharp exhale, I pushed myself off the Horsa.

It was time to start fighting.

3

6th June 1944
00.18 hours

I STAGGERED BACK to the door of the aircraft, which had been slid backwards ready to allow the stream of troops to disembark. It should have been a few feet from the ground, a small jump needed to hop out of it safely but, instead, it was at ground level, a few blades of grass poking up around the bottom edge.

The front wheel had broken off on impact, making us belly slide to a halt, seemingly in some bushes. I looked about foolishly for the wheel, as if finding it and mending it would make my situation somehow marginally better.

I suddenly became very thankful for the fact that there were no anti-glider poles in place. Charlie had become convinced that we would find one impaling us within seconds of hitting French soil, but, from what I could see, there were none. Just a hole here and there ready for them. They should have been in place by tonight, in fact, they should have had explosives rigged to them by now, ready to set off a chain reaction of explosions, finishing us off before we'd even begun. But there were none. I knew Charlie would be thanking God for that one later.

I hoisted myself back up into the main body of the plane and began sifting through the kit of the unconscious men. I checked pulses as I went.

They were all still alive, chins tucked firmly into their chests, just dozing. My eyes were fixed on them for a few moments, like a parent proudly staring at their sleeping children. A gut-wrenching guilt suddenly forced itself upon me, a guilt-ridden realisation that, within the next few minutes, we could all be dead.

Again, this would have been another scenario to add to my comedy of errors, had I not felt like I was completely isolated in enemy territory. Thirty soldiers were in the back of my aircraft, thirty elite soldiers at that, all specially trained in the mission that lay ahead. Instead of having these thirty, heavily armed men standing by my side, I found myself scavenging through their kit in order to free just one other man.

I thrust my hand into one of the bags tucked under a pair of raised legs, as they rested themselves on the opposite bench. Feeling the cold metal of wire cutters, with a sense of relief and accomplishment, I began to withdraw my hand from the bag, I allowed myself a quick exhale of breath which manifested itself as a slight chuckle. Surprised at myself, I quickly put a stop to it.

My throat suddenly constricted as I felt something clamp tightly to it and the unmistakeable feeling of a barrel thrust deep into my gut, a snarling, blackened face staring back at me.

"Friendly, friendly," I moaned in between restricted attempts to breathe. My Adam's apple bobbed up and down rapidly in his hand as I fought earnestly to swallow, a surge of vomit fighting just as hard to find its way out.

The glaring white eyes didn't show any forgiveness; confidence and hatred oozing out of them. His grip tightened around my neck, the barrel digging further into my belly. I felt my skin redden as I resisted the urge to close my eyes and conserve my energy. The hand felt large, large enough to almost make its way right around my neck. It was clammy, I could feel the beads of sweat forming on the surface and seeping into my neck.

I waited for an explosion of pain as a copper bullet punched its way through the barrier of my skin before wreaking havoc in my internal organs, smashing everything into oblivion, no distinction between vital organs and the plinth of wood that it would catapult itself into, on the other side.

I waited for the grip to tighten on me as I lost pint after pint of blood, my killer squeezing every ounce of scarlet liquid from the jerking figure in front of him. My blood would inevitably cascade over the deck of the aircraft, soaking itself into the wooden floorboards that had carried these men into France. My brain began throbbing so hard it felt like it could burst out of my skull at any moment, like a balloon as it began to overinflate before the impending explosion. I could sense my eyes bulging as I began to lose my fight. I waited for the sadistic smile that would send me off from this world and into the next.

I began to experience real fear, like the petrifying fear of finding yourself stranded as a child, without your parents. All my senses were telling me to scream, to let out a shriek that would alert someone of my situation. Even if it was a German. But I couldn't. The oversized hand crushed my voice box, and nothing more than a desperate grunt would come out.

The incredible darkness that I had experienced till this point grew darker still as I began to feel my eyes begin to give in to my attacker.

I was beginning to die.

It was in the back of that Horsa that I began to think about dying. I wondered about the immediate aftermath of my death. Who would find me? Would my killer show any remorse when he discovered who I was?

"Pilot…" I choked, "…Chambers."

I thought of my family. Would I be listed as just another casualty of war? Would they ever find out? I thought of their happy, smiling faces, all staring at me one by one, as they waved me off to war.

I was beginning to accept death.

My body was in the early stages of shutting down and my mind was allowing me to give in. I desperately needed to fight back.

My hand was still firmly placed on the wire cutters, and I tried valiantly to bring them up and out of the bag, in an attempt to bring it crashing down on the skull of my opponent. As my arm retreated from the bag I felt my grip loosen and the cutters clattered to the ground with a humiliating thud.

I tried once more, "John…John Chambers…"

I didn't think he could hear me, and even if he could

hear me, would it register over the anger and malice racing through his body?

Suddenly, his grip released, and the barrel withdrew, causing me to crumple in a heap on the deck, like a discarded piece of food, a glum thump emanating around the cabin.

I thought I heard him apologise, but I was too busy clutching my neck and fighting for oxygen to care. At first, I didn't think I'd ever be able to repay the debt to my lungs, he had clamped down on my throat with such ferocity that I could never imagine my airways fully opening up again. I was surprised at how quickly I was able to suck air in and out again like a normal human being.

As the stars began to fade away from my vision and I gained my senses back, a sudden burning rage overcame me and the intense desire for revenge almost overwhelmed me. Picking myself up, my boots thumped hard on the deck as I made my way over to him. Hearing me coming, he spun round, and immediately I sunk back into myself. The Captain.

In the space of sixty seconds, I went from being bent on revenge, to helping my attacker to assemble his stricken men. Groans and expressions of annoyance became more frequent as slowly, the men began to regain consciousness. Some took longer to come around than others, it was just as well we had a job to do, I had seen how merciless some of these lads could have been when another had been passed out, usually on the way back from another unsanctioned drinking session.

I looked around in relief. I wasn't alone anymore.

The headache intensified as I recovered from my

throttling, my vision almost returning to normal now. My hearing too, had returned, the subdued noises of the world now sounded with clarity. An unexpected benefit of being strangled to within an inch of your life. I could now make out the rich, clear sounds of the world, something I would rather have not had right now. The groans and clinks that resounded were loud, loud enough to be heard by an enemy sentry. We'd need to get going, and fast.

I headed towards the door of the Horsa behind a small paratrooper, I was a good head and shoulders taller than him, and I felt like patting him on the head like a child as he hopped out. As I ducked through the doorway, I paused. I had accepted death. I had got a taste of the pure, terrifying fear of dying. The fear of dying without any of your family or loved ones close by. And yet, in that moment, I had *wanted* to die. I had accepted death as a positive experience, as one that I could look forward to. That scared me more than facing the German guns. The human mind seemed much more powerful in that moment than an enemy bullet.

I made my way back to Charlie and began clipping away at the wires with the heavy, cumbersome cutters, before flinging the loose pieces over my shoulder.

The men took their focus away from cocking their weapons and checking other pieces of their kit for a moment. They hoisted Charlie up as I pulled the last bits of wire from his leg, a satisfying *twang* resounding across the field with each piece. We all stood like statues, as each of them listened for the tell-tale sign of a sentry alerting the garrison. Everyone held their breath in unison with one another, listening as one body. I had done my fair share of listening out already. It was comforting to know I had more ears this time to help me.

Charlie's blood fused with my own, the fresh blood trickling down my arm as the obstruction was removed, glinting in the moonlight as the warm liquid dribbled to the floor.

I dropped the wire cutters to the ground, thumping a small hole into the French countryside, and stretched my hands as they began to cramp up from the intense grip I had subjected them to.

My arms ached from stretching up to untangle Charlie and I swung them up trying to reintroduce blood to them, it was more than likely I would need to use them again soon.

Charlie was laid out flat on his back, before the medic left his duties as a concussion expert and began attending to Charlie's wounds.

We all stood in observation for a moment as Charlie winced while the Doc painfully cleaned each of his wounds with a soft, dabbing motion. His brown, curling hair just poked out from under the rim of his helmet as he squirmed in discomfort while his wounds were sterilised. He began to calm down as some pressure was applied to his wounds and bandages were wrapped tight around him. He even chanced a flash of a smile, he was okay.

The thick layer of sweat was beginning to stick to his face as he got cockier by thrusting his thumb in the air.

"Probably just Grandad's arthritis playing up again," got a chuckle out of a few of us. Charlie retaliated with a few, hushed, character mocking phrases of his own, until the Doc pressed down far too hard on one injury, making Charlie's face return to a mess of screwed up flesh and agonising grunts. I would always wonder if the Doc had done that deliberately, punishing Charlie for being far too confident in that brief moment.

Moonlit faces all glared down at Charlie as we began to block the Doc's light. Ushering us away, we began to disperse slightly and give them a bit more room to work with.

It wasn't until he swung his Sten off his shoulder and hoisted it in front of his waist, pointing it like he was about to mow us all down, that Captain Jenner gave us all a reminder of where we were. His hands, covered in camo paint like the rest of his skin, was threatening to give the game away as they burned a bright red, a side effect, I told myself, of his near murder of the best co-pilot in the regiment.

"Let's go chaps."

He was an unusual character. He took the officer's view of 'them' and 'us' very seriously indeed. No one knew a thing about him. Rumours, as they so often do amongst bored soldiers, flew wildly around that he was married, still only at school when the war broke out and one or two about his serial killings. They were all conjecture, and no one dared ask him any questions about his personal life, even if we were all desperate to know where he'd put the bodies.

When he wasn't wearing his headdress or helmet, his curly locks clung closely to his scalp, as if he was wearing some sort of hair net and his eyes moved in the way someone else would move their lips to convey their emotions. If he was in an aggressive, bad mood, his eyes widened, to the point where they looked as if they would burst. On the other hand, if he smiled, his eyes creased and folded up to the point where they were almost useless.

He rarely smiled though.

He possessed a curious figure, tall and wiry, young, yet far too serious, but not one of us would deny the fact that he was an excellent leader. He kept his distance from us - that much is true - but he would be the first one to volunteer us for extra nights in the field, time he took to take special attention over each of us, spending hours at a time giving company to a sentry, quietly asking probing questions, carefully pondering the answers as he built up individual profiles in his head. I often queried myself as to whether he did this out of a genuine desire to know more about us, or whether he did it to make sure that his sentries stayed awake for the full term of their duty. Either way, he knew full well that the harder we worked, the better trained we were. And, in turn, the better trained we were, the more effective the soldier that he commanded.

More importantly though, as some of the other, more experienced troops pointed out, he was level headed. Something everyone knew would be invaluable once we were in combat. We had all fired live weapons in training, but the thought of someone lining up their sights and firing at me was a completely different story. Level headed was not the response that I was expecting from myself. I needed men like the Captain by my side.

Captain Jenner's understated battle cry was all we needed to prompt us back into being soldiers. I picked up my Sten, clunked a magazine into the well, and cocked the handle.

The freezing steel felt right at home in my sweaty palms as a new wave of confidence swept over me like a tidal wave.

I double checked my weapon was all ready to go by

pulling the cocking handle back half way, to make sure the mag had fed properly. The small nine-millimetre round grinned back at me. It was a small thing, the nine-mil, but it could be just enough to be my saviour, the small nine-millimetre line between life, and death.

My weapon was ready, my mind wasn't. Maybe it was the headache from the throttling I had just received. Maybe it was the fifty-fifty chance that I would be cut down by enemy gunfire before I could get over to the other side of the bridge. I was worried about how easy it would be to defend the bridge to a group of attackers, attackers who were protected only by a thin layer of flesh, rather than a nice thick steel tank to hide behind. All they would have to do was to plonk two machine guns on the far end of the bridge and keep firing until all of us were either lying in a pool of our own blood, or running for our lives towards the beaches like our army had done four years ago. Whatever it was, my head didn't quite seem in it.

Releasing the cocking handle and checking I still had all my spare mags in my bandolier, I gave a short, sharp tug at my battledress, making sure everything was secure. By now I had to give a decent effort to fall in behind the group of men that had begun to stagger groggily towards the bridge.

4

6th June 1944
00.19 hours

I HAD NEVER KNOWN my father in the way that my mother spoke about him and about how he used to be. He had always been a shy man, humble and quiet. He never talked anyone down, and only looked for the best in people. His patience was unconditional, hours spent telling my brother and me to keep away from windows while hammering a football, as hard as was humanly possible, at each other.

He had never once raised his voice at either of us. Never once did he get angry. It got to a point in our childhood, to see how far we could push our father, to make him explode in the same way that we saw so many other fathers tear into their children. This culminated in us performing a great heist from the local shop, numerous bars of chocolate and groceries were stolen, for no other reason than to wind our father up. It became almost like a game to my brother, George, and me, seeing how far we could push him, always wanting to just tip him over the edge. It was never out of a lack of respect for my Dad that my brother and I taunted him, but out of a curiosity that we possessed and a mystery that surrounded him. He was a Dad like no other.

His stern glare was enough to make my brother and I feel as hurt as if we'd been given the belt four or five times, but it never stopped us from looking for trouble.

He had been a confident young man apparently, laughing and joking around with his friends, much the same as me and my brother, always on the lookout for mischief.

He had a youthful glint in his eye, never really wanting to grow up, but always wanting to be around his friends, kicking a ball around and causing havoc. He grew up to become a well-known figure in the village, always up to no good, sourcing this and that for people and bouncing from job to job, but never upsetting anyone. Well, except the local farmers. I supposed it was hereditary, things were never stolen or pinched according to my Dad, merely 'acquired.' The skill of 'acquisition' was an easy one for me to pick up.

My mother often commented on how she feared he would never grow up, stuck in a state of juvenile stupidity. She would smile when telling us about what he was like, the man she fell in love with all those years ago, but the smile would rapidly abandon her face soon after.

They were married during Dad's first leave after he signed up, the most mature and grown up thing he had ever done it seemed. Mum knew that what was to come would be hell, but it would be better for him if he knew he had something to try and come home for, an empty house is enough to make anyone suicidal. Increasingly, I felt like I would now be doomed to that fate.

The story never went much further than that. The comments about his maturity went from a "childish stupidity" to "never the same." Mum never pushed herself to tell me, I don't think she ever wanted me to know. She blamed the war for the change in my Dad, she never told me, but the day I volunteered, I saw it in her eyes. She had retreated into the kitchen silently, a broken, despairing woman. But she'd known I had to do it.

Never once had she shed a tear when talking about my Dad, never once had she shown any overtly visible signs of grief for the man she mourned. But the effect that it had had on her mind, the piece of *her* that had remained over in France with my Dad, was far more haunting than any of her tears.

I longed to know what he was like before, I wanted *him* as my Dad. It killed me to see him like he was, a young, fun and exciting young man locked in the body of a man who had seen too much and sacrificed a great deal.

Not long after I'd signed up, I found myself being subjected to a story of another war, a distant one. The one my Dad had experienced. From the moment he started to tell me I desperately wanted to know more but at the same time, prayed that it would end. He'd only spoken to me about it once, and that was enough. I couldn't listen to anymore, he couldn't tell me anymore.

He sat in his chair and I looked up as he grunted in discomfort. He played around with his pipe before striking a match and lighting it. The chemical cocktail of odours that wafted to my nostrils of the match was swiftly replaced by the sweet aroma of tobacco. Pipes had never been my style, I much preferred cigarettes, American cigarettes.

"Through mud and blood to the green fields beyond," he scoffed, his pipe bobbing up and down like a piston as he spoke.

"That was our motto…but there were no green fields."

I shifted uncomfortably in my seat. I was used to him speaking to me, but this seemed more like the ramblings of a mad man. I went back to reading my book, one half recommended to me by another recruit, as "alright, but a bit wet."

I looked up as he continued to speak, more to his pipe than to me, staring into the bowl and allowing the smoke to permeate through his eyes. I did not know what had triggered this sudden recollection of his military service, whether it was because of me recently having signed up, or if it was down to the fact that I had just celebrated my twenty-first birthday and he now considered me grown up enough to learn about my old man.

"I joined the Army Service Corps. 1916." That already doubled what I knew about his wartime experiences. I loved my dad, he was my hero in many ways, calmly, quietly, persevering with his life, despite all the problems that he had. I looked at him out of respect rather than intrigue, it felt like the right thing to do, I hadn't even finished my chapter.

I was more interested in the vast amount of smoke that continued to rise from his pipe, and disappear into the great valleys that now formed on his forehead.

His voice seemed to fade in and out, he spoke so softly,

and I began to get the impression that I was missing words on either side of his sentences.

He still peered into his pipe, like a schoolboy avoiding eye contact with his teacher, not wanting to be selected to give an unknown answer. Deep sighs began to break up his speech. Either he didn't want to go on, or the smoke was getting into his lungs.

"The tank was slow, cumbersome, vulnerable. A bit like you in your first year of school." His speech was broken up by a haunting chuckle, making me feel like running from the room, but I couldn't, I was transfixed.

He cupped his hand over his mouth and, for a moment, I thought he was going to vomit. He held it there as he shut his eyes gently, as if he was trying to focus all his energy on remembering something.

"It looked awful, it was rough, bits stuck out of it as if it was half finished and it made you giddy with all the fumes," a reminiscent smile appeared on his face, causing the valleys to appear on his cheeks as well as at the corner of his eyes.

He spoke slowly, deliberately, but involuntary pauses broke his speech up so much I wondered if we would ever reach the end of what he was trying to tell me. In a way, I was more comfortable with that.

I thought for a moment about re-engaging myself in my book, hoping that he would eventually realise that he was speaking, rather than thinking, and he would supress his speech and place it firmly back in his mind. Smoke shot out of his nostrils as he smirked, and for the first time he looked up from the smoke and across at me, but the sadness in his eyes made me wish for a pipe of my own. I busied myself repositioning my body in the chair.

"But it was a thing of beauty. It glided over the ground, nothing stopped it, it didn't look as though it should get anywhere, a twenty-nine-tonne steel box Johnny, it don't make sense, does it?"

The tone in his voice rose, and steadily grew faster as the fire in his eyes was stoked.

His eyes began to fill with tears, but I was more concerned about whether he was expecting a response from me. He held my gaze for a moment longer, softly nodding his head up and down with the occasional mutter in between puffs.

"We were at the forefront of a technological war, son. *We* were the ones that every man on the Western Front wanted on his side. They relied on us, they would watch us as rounds pinged off the side of our armour as if they were peas."

He smirked at his own joke again. His speech and demeanour was proud, something I had never seen in him before, arrogant almost, but it was combatted by humbling tears that glistened in his eyes.

"*Gott mit uns* is what they had on their belts," he paused momentarily as the cogs whirred in his head, trying to translate.

"But our boys in their dugouts had a sign themselves. *'God with them. Tank with us.'*"

He sat in silence for a few minutes, just watching the smoke that billowed from his pipe. I began to settle back down to my book.

"There were eight of us in our tank. Six beasts in our section. We were to smash through the enemy lines and advance on the nearby town."

He couldn't remember the name anymore, no matter how hard he massaged his forehead.

"We were the most advanced soldiers on the battle-field. We cut down *everything*. And do you know who they sent in behind us to clean up? The cavalry. Horses were cut down all around us, Johnny. Not a thing we could do.

"We'd see 'em die, that was bad enough, great beasts rearing up as they took machine gun rounds to their chest, before thumping to the ground in agony. But the smell was worse. No one cleared them up, Johnny. Eighty-odd stone of horse meat, just rotting all around us. It smells okay at first, just a sweet aroma, but before long the flies attack, it begins to rot, flooding the area with a nostril burning substance…"

He was speaking in a matter-of-fact manner, as if it did not affect him but, before long, his voice trailed off as splutters turned to blubbing.

Leave it. Your job is to stay alive now.

As the sound of my Dad's uncontrollable sobbing faded back into the pits of my mind, the sound of clinking kit began to take over. I pushed myself harder to catch up with the others.

5

6th June 1944
00.20 hours

THE RHYTHMIC CHIMING of my kit rubbing itself up and down my body was almost hypnotic, it felt heavier every time it fell and threatened to pull me to the ground.

My breathing was in sync with the clinking of my kit, as were my footsteps. I became a machine, all the cogs working in unison together as I paced my way towards the bridge.

My feet began to itch as the terrible woollen socks began to soak themselves in the dampness of the night, and I felt great clumps of my foot cling nastily to the fibres of the wool.

The outline of the men in front of me soon changed from silhouettes to machines themselves as the dull jingling of kit echoed from every direction.

A constant tinging, swishing sound began to flow across the field, as all of us moved as one body towards our target. My Sten slipped around in my hands as the sweat threatened to loosen my grip on my weapon, but my new-found confidence made sure I had a tight grip on it. I felt unstoppable. A fully automatic weapon swaying around at my hip, surrounded by like-minded and similarly armed men all powering towards a few, unsuspecting, hopefully sleepy soldiers. Nothing would stop us. We were trained and ready for combat. This is what we had all waited for. This is what all the months of training was for, the endless night exercises and constant classroom lessons. All of it coming together in what should be a few moments of pure aggression and total surprise.

I pushed all other thoughts out of my mind; my socks, Charlie, even my Dad. They were all gone. It was just me, my Sten and the enemy. All meanderings about failure or the idea of our inequality with the enemy simply disappeared. There was no possibility of failure in my mind, no chance even, of me being killed.

My helmet bobbed around on my head, like a child whose clothes don't fit him properly. I couldn't shake the clamminess from my hands, no matter how confident I felt, and I allowed them to slide all over the steel.

I was nearing the bridge, getting closer to where my life could possibly be cut short. And I found myself running. Saliva splashed from my mouth as I began charging forwards, allowing it to cling to my chin as it was soon joined by more.

I stopped sprinting suddenly and felt my heels dig into the French countryside, leaving great craters where I halted. The unmistakeable *crack crack crack* of a Sten gun blast resounded out, breaking the rhythmic pounding of footsteps on grass.

My silence had been broken.

"Keep going!" someone screamed as he charged past me, another grabbing my webbing and thrusting me forward. I stumbled as he released me from his grip and flew past me, struggling to keep my legs galloping towards potential death.

Here we go. This is it. This is what you trained for.

Minutes before I had been a master of the air, toying with the glider and manipulating nature to guide my craft down gently alongside Charlie. Nothing else mattered now. I was a soldier.

I felt alone all of a sudden, as if one enemy soldier had me in his sights, tracing my every movement ready to pull the trigger. I could see myself slow down as he steadied his breathing, getting ready to take the shot that would cut me down. The loneliness was combatted by my certainty that every man that I could see charging towards the bridge, shared my every thought.

I rounded the corner from the field and the crunching of boots on a more solid track became audible. The crunching of boots gave me a new wave of confidence. I was no longer slipping over the sodden grass, but I had a firm footing in France.

The large, imposing structure of the steel bascule bridge rose up in front of me, as if it was only just being sketched out onto an artist's pad. The closer I got to it, the more detailed the sketch got, and extra features began to appear. I wanted to stop and marvel at it, it was unlike any other bridge I had ever seen before.

To my right, some men that I didn't recognise, but

definitely on my side, leapt out of a trench looking more than pleased with themselves, two German grenades each sticking proudly out of their breast pockets. They wouldn't need to bother reading the instruction manual with those ones. We knew how almost every weapon in the Reich worked, with our eyes closed. All you had to do with the potato masher grenade was unscrew the cap at the base of the handle, let the small porcelain ball dangle out from the bottom of it and give it an almighty tug. You then had five seconds to get rid of it before you splattered yourself all over the countryside. The two men shared a joke with each other before shaking hands and charging onwards.

Preparing to die was one lesson that we hadn't been given as part of our training. So, I did the next best thing, prepare to go down fighting, the voice of one of our lecturers ringing in my head.

"To go down with a full magazine is to go down a coward. An empty magazine secures hero status, gents."

Making it to the start of the bridge, I brought my Sten up into my shoulder, ready to fire. It was safe to say that none of us here were going for hero status, we just wanted to make it out of here alive; but not one of us wanted to go down with the possibility of being called a coward.

The vicinity erupted with a clamour as weapons were fired at invisible targets and men screamed orders to each other. Great zipping noises became the incessant background to my soundtrack of war, each zip sounding closer and closer to my head.

Flashes of light sparked up on the other side of the bridge and I prepared myself to open fire, aiming just above the bursts of gunfire.

"Move!" came the command, "They've got charges all over! Get to the other side!"

Men all around pushed themselves up from their knees and, weapons raised, began charging towards the other side of the bridge. We poured across the great steel structure, footsteps creating a gunfire of their own as they clanged their way across. Men jostled with each other, as if a great stampede was on in order to see the King.

I felt a pop of air against my leg, almost as if someone had spat onto my trouser leg, a worrying sign that a bullet had come dangerously close to embedding itself inside me. I felt amazing, I had avoided death so far, I was still living when so many men, generations before me, had perished within a matter of seconds. I felt completely invincible, as if each bullet smacked into a defensive barrier around me and yet, simultaneously, I had never felt quite so aware of my own mortality.

I glanced across at one of the slit trenches. A machine gun hung limply on a mount where, if manned, it would point directly down the road. On the far side a small figure sat cowering in the corner. He was one of us that was for sure, his face blackened with the same cream issued to all of us. He clutched his rifle passionately as he muttered to himself.

Tears cascaded down his cheeks as he uttered what I could only imagine was some sort of prayer.

"Poor devil," I found myself murmuring as another *whizz-crack* pushed my legs faster to the other side of the bridge.

My senses seemed to sharpen with every snap of a gun, able to take in new information quicker than a machine gun can spit out its deadly cargo. Something whizzed past my cheek, like a bee who flies a little too close to you, just able to feel the tickle of his furry back. I thought about the bullet as it continued on its journey, wondering whether some other poor man would feel it plunge itself into his flesh.

That one didn't have my name on it. None of them seemed to. According to the Colonel, it wasn't the one with my name on it that I had to worry about, but the one with 'To Whom it may Concern' scratched into it that should really get me quaking.

The eruption of noise all around me didn't seem real, there was less sound on the rifle range when twenty men all fired weapons at once. This was more than twenty men this time, way more.

A pressure wave suddenly assaulted my ears, like they had been cupped and a fist had slammed into the side of it. My right ear popped again, and a high-pitched squeal rang out for a moment or two, before subsiding. I knew immediately what it was. Grenade. I didn't know who had thrown it, or if it had even been a friend or foe. All I knew was that the grenade had one purpose. To kill. It would shatter into a thousand pieces, lethal darts of metal flying in every direction, trying to maim if the initial blast had not got you first.

I had seen first-hand what it could do to a man. One recruit, had shards of molten metal embedded into his legs within the first few weeks of training because he was on the wrong end of a grenade, no one had seen the poor man after that, apparently being consigned to a desk job, for the sake of the training teams, for the duration of the war.

My heart was racing, I waited for the moment where I would lose my footing, the bridge collapsing all around me, sending me into the freezing midnight waters below, and that was if I wasn't instantly killed by the blast.

The blast never came, but the pinging of rounds as they ricocheted off the bridge intensified as I pounded my way over the river.

I raised my weapon as I surged forwards and discharged a magazine into the oncoming flashes in front of me; at least now if I was to go down, it was as a hero and not, as was feared by so many, a coward. I hurtled forwards so fast it crossed my mind that I might even run into one of my own rounds if I was not careful. My pace slowed as I changed mags, but my gaze was never diverted from what lay directly ahead of me. I knew exactly where everything was, I'd trained and retrained to the point where I could storm this bridge with my eyes shut.

The Sten bucked and kicked as it wrestled to break free from my clammy grip, the heat from the discarded rounds almost searing my skin as they jumped from the weapon. It was unlikely that any of these rounds was going to shorten the war too dramatically, the likelihood of them even hitting a target so small, in fact, that it was probably better to save my rounds, but, it felt good, like I was making some sort of difference.

I knew there would be a few buildings when we got to the other side that we would need to clear, a few reinforced trenches with a couple of machine guns and hopefully only a handful of men to deal with. But that wasn't my priority right now. My priority was to get off this bridge as soon as possible, then find some cover and hopefully, I wouldn't be the only man to make it across.

I slotted the magazine in neatly, pulled the cocking handle and picked up my pace. I was only a few strides away from the end of the bridge now. A few men were in front of me, pulsing forward just as fast and as enthusiastic as me. I watched as a round entered a man's chest, stopping him dead in his tracks and catapulting him backwards. I carried on past him just as he began screaming out in agony and clutching at the void that now occupied his chest.

Three men huddled over a figure on my left and as I sped past I caught a glimpse of metallic blood, pooling itself on the chilled steel. The scarlet liquid that had not so long ago occupied its owner's veins, was now spilling out of him quicker than if a canteen of water had been upended. I didn't need to stop; the others were doing their job.

I heard each, individual echo of my rounds, above everything else, as they hit the buildings around me. Another empty magazine now occupying my gun, I slammed myself up against the wall of the nearest building so hard that I felt the wall wobble slightly. I took a few moments to catch my breath and wiped away the saliva that congealed around my chin. I wheezed as my lungs tried desperately to draw in oxygen, a sharp pain emanating from my chest with every inhalation.

I placed my hands on my knees and dropped my weapon to the floor gently.

"You're as useful as a dead man while that weapon is on the floor," a voice grunted in my direction as he joined me at the wall.

He handed it to me as we were joined by some other muddy faces, all panting and wheezing just like me, fighting each other for the shared air around us.

"This is all rather exciting isn't it chaps," I couldn't

quite work out the face, he had no features like the rest of us, but his voice gave him away. Lieutenant Maxwell was a likeable officer, but he was one who had the innate ability to get on one's nerves. This was one of those moments, we all ignored him.

A string of curse words echoed around us, and I prepared to see a bloodied body being dragged towards us, needing my medical attention. He avoided clattering into the wall as the rest of us had done, stopping short. Hopping up and down in anticipation, he undid his trousers and let them drop to the ground. He laughed nervously as he relieved himself up the side of the wall, great pillars of steam and a strong stench evaporating around us.

The noise of utter relief seemed to resound louder than the clamour of machine guns had ever done.

"Who needs a radio when you can rely on Jimmy and his smoke signals?" The others all chortled in unison as Jimmy finished up.

"I've been holding that in since we left Tarrant," he apologised, pulling his trousers up, embarrassed, "the Lieutenant wouldn't let me go out the door. Something about giving our mission away!"

"I was more concerned that it would turn into an unsanctioned bombing run, if you get my drift lads!" came the mocking reply from the Lieutenant.

I was relieved for Jimmy, but it was a relief that we all needed before we started the next phase of the operation.

A calmness began to descend on the area. A few shouts went up every now and then as the injured were pulled back. A grenade or two went off as machine gun nests were destroyed. This was the kind of silence that I was used to, and in fact, preferred. I let my mind wander for a moment or two, allowing myself a brief respite to the world I found myself in.

All of a sudden, what seemed like a demented and ecstatic town crier began screaming and shouting as he charged up and down the street. As he did so he was met with whoops and cheers.

"Ham and Jam! Ham and lovely, wonderful, British, Jam!"

He was cut short by the eruption of gunfire.

6

20th November 1917
05.30 hours

THE MARK IV TANK. That was my fortress. My heavy-handed beast. The Ugly Duckling.

The cartoon of a small duckling with great buck teeth and cross eyes was a comical sight to see sprawled out across the side of a quarter inch thick, khaki coloured armour plating. It was even more comical when bullets started ricocheting off his teeth and large projectiles erupted from its guns. The colours had faded in the poor weather, but the basic outline of our lucky mascot was still intact, framed by a spattering of bullet holes and dents.

It lurched around like a bull as we drove, making every attempt to throw you off its back but at the same time charging forwards like an Olympic sprinter. It was slower and much more cumbersome than a sprinter, but it did its job. We were just her passengers.

There were eight of us in our original crew. Ten if you include the two six-pound guns hanging out of the sides, ready to spray death and destruction on all those that blocked it.

That's if we ever got close enough to the frontline. The interior of our tank reached melting point so frequently that we often felt as though we would pass out, the exhaust pipes sat just inches away from all of us and glowed a vibrant red as we maxed out the engine, pushing it further and further each time.

The fumes were encompassing, no real separation between us and the dirty air that intoxicated the inside of the tank, no mask could ever protect us from that. It was one of the reasons I had bought my pipe, I figured that adding slightly to the fumes while at the same time gracing myself with a nicer aroma was worthwhile, a sentiment which wasn't exactly shared with the rest of my crew.

But the fumes from my pipe and that of our beloved tank, really were the least of our worries. The engine was prone to giving out at any moment, with no hint of its desperation or unwillingness to continue. The grinding and chugging of the engine, as it dragged us forward, would just stop. We would all stare at each other in a brief moment of unbelief and quite often, relief. It meant we wouldn't be going into battle today.

It was also cramped and uncomfortable, to the point where I kept my helmet on at all times after giving myself a lump on the side of my head during my initial experiences in her, something that I never fully got used to. You could smack the side of your fist against any part of her structure and you wouldn't hear the clang that you might expect from steel, just a solid, dependable, thud.

We had to rub our bodies up against each other in order to squeeze past one another, but we devised a very nifty loading up routine to minimise the bodily contact, something that we, as a crew, were incredibly proud of.

I was in love though, we all were, and, like any obliging man in a relationship, the issues and problems that she gave us, were overlooked. We loved her, our Doris, so did the troops that we saw all around us, waving us on as we took the fight to the enemy. They had an unwavering faith in her, in us, to protect them, to give the enemy a nasty surprise when they saw a steel monster slowly trundling its way towards them.

1917 had been my last battle, the last one on the Western Front anyway, the last time that Doris would take me towards my objective, alongside almost four hundred other ugly beasts. Four hundred other tanks and yet it would be the loneliest that I had ever felt. The most vulnerable.

I couldn't pinpoint an exact reason for why I felt so lonely, I just always seemed to be before an advance. It seemed odd, to feel lonely, in a small, steel container with seven other men, all tightly packed in together. Thousands of men outside the steel box sat in their dugouts, willing us on, cheering us on. All these men on my side and yet, on the inside, I felt completely void of any company. It didn't seem like it was the best place for your head to be before a battle.

I often found myself thinking about Rorke's Drift, where the men had been outnumbered by almost twenty to one and questioned whether they had felt as lonely as I did, before debating with myself as to whether I had the right to feel lonely compared to them. Then I reminded myself that my enemy, had machine guns and artillery, not antique rifles and assegai spears.

We all sat in the tank and waited; waited for the seconds to tick round and signal the advance. No one spoke, that was the most haunting thing, all we seemed capable of doing was staring. The noises of the outside world were shut off by the quarter inch thick armour, a mere rumble of the life we knew, just the other side of the steel. A few coughs every now and then, and a mumbled prayer from Don, one of the gear men. He spoke with a lisp, something that always seemed rather cruel seeing as his surname was Somersville, which is why he was insistent on his first name only being used, a request which the Lieutenant, couldn't quite get his head around. Don was from Northern Ireland, which made my understanding of what he said, even worse, but what I did know, is that before this particular advance, he had lost his picture of his girlfriend, something which made his already short fuse, even shorter. We knew absolutely nothing about her, he had a picture of her, but none of us had ever seen it. It was odd, all of us had shared everything about our lives, you had to, even Lieutenant Harper had delved into his background. Don however, kept himself to himself.

I stared at the great levers that leapt from the floor, the levers that, pushed in the right direction, would drive us to our deaths. We waited and waited before we heard the rumble of the other engines firing up.

Ours was fired up too, and as it was, I yanked a piece of cloth over my mouth, shamefully stolen from a dead man's battle shirt. I had taken it from him after my first piece of action in Doris, the fumes had made me so giddy that I had been on the verge of asking someone else to take over as I couldn't see straight. I wrapped it around my lower face and neck and tied it in front of my mouth, giving a futile bit of protection from the deathly fumes. The fumes she gave off would catch you on the back of your throat, leading to a few hours of great, whooping coughs and a monumental sore throat. Some of the lads who had operated on tanks for a while longer than us, were even known to have coughed up specks of blood.

With a swift jerk of the lever, we lurched off, the tracks squeaking as they began to warm themselves up, tirelessly wrapping their way around us, propelling us forward.

We drove in silence for twenty minutes, maybe more, before Lieutenant Harper, a young, but already experienced officer told us we were coming up to No Man's Land. He slammed his peep hole shut, opting instead for the miniscule periscope that courageously poked its way out from the front of the tank. Not wishing to have a lot of machine gun rounds embedded firmly into my face, I snapped mine shut too.

Suddenly, I felt a lack of resistance in the controls and it felt as if we had got airborne for a moment as we trickled over the British trench, a deathly silence was pierced only by the low rumblings and squeaks of the tanks.

I thought about the chaps below us dejectedly for a moment or two. I could feel them all, helmets all ducked down low below the parapet as we trundled over, not knowing what was before them. Some would be praying no doubt, others thinking of home and loved ones, while others still would be hoping optimistically of returning home again to their old lives. Soon though, and I'm sure most of them realised it, their lives would be cut short by the brutal reality of No Man's Land, as rounds from every side and direction would cut them down one by one.

We'd seen it all multiple times before, it would be the same this time and the same again next time. I was slowly becoming accustomed to watching men's limbs being ripped off their body by the round of a *maschinengewehr*.

I wondered about how much of the war they had seen so far. Some had been lucky, or unlucky, and made it through almost three years of war, I wasn't naïve though, I knew for certain that for a lot of these boys, it would be the first, and the last time, that they ventured out into No Man's Land. Without a doubt, a small part of every man in the offensive would die today.

Within a matter of seconds, the trenches were behind us and, so too were the thought of the thousands of khaki uniforms all crouching below the parapet. It was just Doris and her crew now. The other tanks all faded to the periphery of my mind. We were all that mattered now. I would only worry about the rounds being directed towards us from here on in.

It didn't take long for the sounds of guns opening fire to permeate through the thick steel. At first, they seemed far away, far too distant to worry about, more pot shots than directed rounds, being acutely aware though, that even the vaguest shot could get lucky, I kept my wits about me.

We rose and fell as if we were in the Navy, riding the waves as we steamed across the ocean and I felt a sudden affinity to my brother. He had been in the Navy and saw action at Jutland, where he had lost his life. We didn't know much about the way Harry had died, just that, he had. I couldn't help but imagine the way that he had come to the end of his life. Had he died in agony as his burning ship began to sink? Had he died instantly from the explosion of a torpedo? Or had he drowned in peace and tranquillity?

It led to the natural progression of how I was to die, for I surely was, and whether or not my family would ever find out the truth about my demise.

I pulled myself away from that image as we jolted into the bottom of a water-filled shell hole. I wondered if there was anything living in this one, rats, lice, German soldiers, Brit—

The artillery round exploded to our left, sending a vibration up my body, through the controls. I fought with Doris for a moment as we were sent up onto our right track, just as all the other guns opened up on the Western Front, all of them pinging fiery rounds towards us.

We recoiled slightly as one of our six pounders ejected its cargo, quickly followed by the other gun to my right. The rhythmic thumping of our guns, mixed with the sound of our fellow tanks, became almost therapeutic. I always felt more at ease when we could return fire, it gave me the false hope that it meant the enemy had their head down, more concerned with preserving their own life than taking mine. In reality, I knew, that our six-pound rounds were probably flying high over the frontline trench and smashing into an unoccupied reserve trench or connecting line. Either way, it made me feel better, it helped me to keep the tank going forward, and not throwing Doris around and heading for home.

As we trundled across No Man's Land, I found myself

chuckling at the strange irony of giving a male tank a woman's name. It comforted us all to have a female name to take to war, almost as if our mothers had come to join in with us.

Lighter rounds began pinging off the side of our beast, as if pebbles were being dropped violently into a pan. The tinging intensified to a crescendo as we drew more attention than if we'd parked Doris in Trafalgar Square. Lieutenant Harper, sat right next to me, was barely audible as he barked for the machine gunners to open up. I couldn't tell if they'd heard him, they were firing anyway. He forgot we had been here before.

Sweat poured down from my brow and was soaked up into the fabric of my pathetic mask. It had begun to taste salty and oily and I had to regularly spit into it to stop myself from swallowing the fumey cocktail. I tore it from my face as it began to irritate my skin and let it dangle around my neck. I could feel great lumps and blotches on the surface of my face, and I just knew they would be a glowing red colour, they always were. It's how I got the nickname 'Wilhelm' from the rest of my crew, thanks to a chilling resemblance to the Kaiser in several comedic drawings of the man in many newspapers. But the discomfort of not being able to breathe properly and the inevitable ridicule would be the price I'd pay.

The incessant racket screaming from the engine seemed to grow louder than ever before and began to cloud my mind. The intense noise contributed significantly to a huge pressure bursting from my skull, I needed fresh air, and soon.

The tinging grew louder and louder as furious bees whizzed past, slamming themselves suicidally into us.

"Hold tight!" I found myself screaming, as I felt resistance in the controls while the tracks struggled to crush the barbed wire.

As we shook our way over the German lines, it was impossible to block out the thoughts of the men below. They were the enemy, the very people that we had been taught to hate, to kill. But I couldn't help but feel a sympathy for them, all of them there with their individual characteristics and foibles. In many ways, they were just like us, I supposed. Yes, they were killers, murderers even, but with their heads ducking down as a thirty-tonne steel box trundled over their positions, they became just like our boys, who would more than likely be dead within a couple of days, if not, hours.

The sound of multiple twangs freed up the controls and we lurched forward with a renewed energy towards the enemy stronghold. We were to continue forwards to a nearby town where we would hold and wait for reinforcements.

The noise of war died down as we squeaked our way through the French countryside. We stopped just short of the edge of a sparse forest.

The Lieutenant risked opening the hatch.

He muttered and cursed under his breath as he drew his pistol and leapt out of the tank, leaving the door wide open as he stormed out.

We jumped out behind him, drawing and readying our revolvers.

"Where is everyone?!"

I looked around nervously, there wasn't a soul about. Not even any enemy. The Mark IV was an incredible contraption, a real technological miracle; the vision it allowed its occupants however, meant that it wouldn't be taking tourists around London anytime soon. We hadn't been able to see any of our other tanks.

We were able to talk freely, but out of fear, we rasped to each other. I kept my eyes fixed firmly on the trees, willing them to move so I could empty a cylinder load of rounds into the nearest moving object. My finger twitched as it precariously rested on the trigger. I made the conscious decision to remove my index finger for now, I didn't want to make this situation even worse by accidentally sticking a round into one of my mate's backs.

"We can't be the only ones left."

We staggered around for a while, circling Doris and hoping that at any moment we would hear the familiar squeal of tracks as they homed in to find us.

As Lieutenant Harper put his binoculars away for the seventh time, we all came to the realisation that we were alone. Don was already praying, his lisping tongue probably praying more for the return of his photograph than to get us lot out alive. He never had his priorities right.

Four hundred tanks and this is it. Just eight men.

"They've either gone on ahead or retreated. We have two options; we go back and risk a breakdown in enemy held territory…" he looked at us for a response, which he didn't get, "…or proceed to the objective, which is closer, in the hope that they *have* made it there before us. Thoughts?"

We all had thoughts, all of them the same. We all wanted to go home. I couldn't see how anyone could have overtaken us, we had pushed Doris to her absolute limit, we had led the charge, then suddenly, we had found ourselves alone. There was no chance of us being lost, we had all seen the route, and the Lieutenant had never once let us down in his navigation.

Or was today his first balls up?

"I say we carry on chaps."

There was no further discussion, we all had differing opinions of this situation, some more democratic than others, but we all chose not to voice them, most of our suggestions would have been wholesomely unhelpful. One by one we hopped back into our steel tank and began rolling our way forward once more.

We began to edge forward precariously, and I could sense that each one of us was holding our breath, and not because of the fumes. We knew we were now completely alone.

Out of my peep hole I could see a dense mist as it began to descend, like a blanket being pulled up and over the terrain around us. It clung to the ground, and wrapped its way around the trees that had now begun to flank us. In my mind I watched figures dance between the trees like children. In reality though, I knew that any figures in amongst the trees would almost certainly not be playful children.

I kept my eyes dead ahead, not because that's the only place I could look, but because I didn't much want to see the hordes of men pour from the forest around us, and descend on us like circling vultures. As I began to take notice of the cloud, our pace dropped rapidly, the engine began to scream, filling the interior with a fog thicker than that outside.

Eventually, the engine gave up with a depressing whine.

"No! No! No!" Screamed Harper, as he ordered four of us out, to scout and secure the area.

The two rifles we had stored away were snatched up leaving me with just a revolver. As Jack, our resident mechanic got to work on the beast, the four of us spread out. He was another one with a short fuse, something of a recurring theme inside our tank, and we knew that when he was working, it was best to leave him well alone, besides, he loved Doris more than he loved his own mother.

We were in a wooded area, one that had obviously been cleared to allow vehicles and men to pass through easily. The beaten track that we were driving on had hoof marks mixed with foot prints in the sodden mud. I could just make out the individual foot prints of boots as they had been retreating in the very direction we were now heading. Crouching down I tried to guess what size boot the possessor of this particular footprint had. Roughly the same as mine I supposed. I pulled my own boot from the clutches of the enemy's footprint as I begun to swivel round and take in the rest of our surroundings.

On either side of the wide path were banks, maybe four-foot-high, where the trees and forestry had continued to grow as if there was no war on. It was from here that I was half expecting the German army to emerge from, mowing us all down in the process. Heaving myself up using the flimsy root of a nearby tree, I crouched behind a sturdy trunk to continue taking in my environment.

This was not a good place to break down in a tank, if there ever was a good one. The track continued out in front of us, but rose gently, which made it more difficult for us to see what lay ahead of us, even with the Lieutenant's trusty binoculars. The amount of traffic that had clearly been using this road was not a good sign for a lone tank either. It meant that either a secondary defensive position was up ahead, or a regrouping point for a potential counter attack.

The one thing that I couldn't help but noticing was the distinct lack of any kind of mechanised tank tracks. I decided to keep that one to myself, as I was sure the others had already spotted it for themselves.

I watched as my crewmates hoisted themselves up the bank as well, the two rifles slightly further up than us lowly, revolver bearing men. I knew I could trust them, I'd been with them a while, we'd been in this situation together many times before. But that didn't necessarily make it any easier.

The track they had made was desolate, other than the churned-up earth and footprints. Up here, it couldn't have been more different. I hadn't seen so much green this close to the frontline since being in France. A scattering of Blue-bells had sprung up not too far from my resting point, only a handful of them nearby, the main gathering of them stretching much further into the woods, like a prettier version of Hansel and Gretel. The lilac glow of the bell drooped softly at the top of the stem, almost as if it was dying, but its colour aggressively contradicting that.

The silence was shocking, if it hadn't filled me with a sense of dread and paranoia, I would have relished in it. It was so quiet, I could just imagine the birds singing softly in the trees before the war had begun. As I reminisced about birdsong, I yearned to know where all the birds on the Western Front had gone, for I had not seen one, not even a blackbird, for some time.

I pined to see one, just one, emerge from the treetops

and I found myself muttering encouragement to a bird that I knew wasn't there. I could barely remember what they looked like anymore. A sudden urge to want to fly, to be able to glide over the treetops gripped me with such ferocity that I couldn't ignore it. Maybe I would learn to fly one day.

I slid down the tree, in a brief moment of relaxation. I sucked in the clean air, a marked difference from the grease filled oxygen I had been breathing in for the last hour, maybe this breakdown would do me some good after all. My hand slipped over my forehead as the black sweat that clung to my head rubbed off on my hand.

I let out a groan as the release of oxygen unsuspectingly passed over my vocal chords and, closing my eyes, I allowed myself to risk thinking of home. I had enjoyed many hours in Thetford forest with my wife. I had not been able to call her my wife for too long, but now I did at every given opportunity, every man in the British Army knew who I was and how long we had been married. We'd sit much like I was now, back to the tree, listening intently to the different warbles of the birds of the trees, identifying each one in turn.

We could sit for hours in total silence, content only with each other's company, able to drink in and bask in the total silence and yet, feel closer to one another for it.

I urged the birds to sing now, just one solitary tweet would fill my soul with the peace and reassurance that I craved, but nothing came. I could hardly remember what they all sounded like, I could hardly remember home.

I sighed. Simultaneously, a great yell shattered the sacred silence.

7

6th June 1944
00.21 hours

BRICK DUST and mortar sprayed into my mouth as rounds began chipping away at the building like a furious sculptor. I marvelled at the terrific light display that was exploding all around me, great flashes of light as lightning-quick fire-flies zipped around the small village. With each crack of a gun, a person would be lit up, sometimes just a head, other times a full figure, but each time enough to see a man pulling the trigger. Voices yelled and grunted in all the directions I could comprehend, as the figures fought with the raging bulls that wrestled in their shoulders.

I was yanked backwards by my webbing by an unknown pair of hands standing behind me, the hands belonging to a body that threw itself in front of me and onto the ground. Before I really knew what had happened, three round bursts were spitting their way out from the Bren gun, standing proudly on the bipod, butt kicking away into the shoulder of my rescuer. I loved the Bren, the power and courage that you felt when operating a small gun, like a revolver, was powerful enough, but one that was able to relinquish five hundred rounds in sixty seconds, gave me such a sense of satisfaction that I would forget the devastation it could cause. I stared at him for a moment or two, like a little boy who had just stumbled into his favourite football player.

He rolled over on to his side to gain a little extra cover as lethal shards of stone were thrown up in the air by retaliating rounds. He fumbled in his back pocket for another magazine, the dust cloud that had formed around us from the brick seemed to be sucked directly into his lungs as he turned and screamed at me.

"House over the crossroads…upstairs window, MG, take it now!" His voice was so strained I thought it might give up if he uttered another syllable. He coughed and spluttered for a moment, before splashing a lump of brick dust red phlegm on the ground beside him, ushering me away with his hands.

The noise intensified and battered my senses as he pinged a few more rounds in the direction of the machine gun, my signal to move. I found myself sprinting for my life again, no other thoughts passing through my mind other than sending one foot crashing down in front of the other. A stabbing pain shot up my leg as I brought one leg down harder than I needed to, but within a millisecond it was flying through the air once more, before it clattered to the ground. It was a process that I had to consciously push myself to continue doing.

The sound of the suicidal wasps and the energetic fireflies disappeared, replaced only by the rushing of the wind as I charged across the open space, with no final destination, until a pile of sandbags came into view. I slid my way behind them in a fashion that a professional footballer would be proud of, clattering into the stomach of a trooper who was holed up there.

I nodded a "sorry" to him before we began to pool our knowledge of the situation. We had charged across the bridge in a westward direction, the road following in that direction before splitting and heading north and south. Just off to the right of the junction, a solitary building overlooked the crossroad, where the shutters of an upstairs window had been thrown open to reveal a sandbagged machine gun.

I spat on the ground to compose myself, to clear my mind as well as my throat, which was producing much more saliva than I could cope with. He did the same, but allowed a sliver of it to dangle, before wrapping its way under his chin, like a cobweb. It wasn't the sort of thing that I would do under normal circumstances, but these were anything but normal circumstances; I was about to charge full pelt towards a weapon that could spit out over twelve hundred rounds a minute.

The only way of getting there was another Olympic sprinter impression, an Olympic sprinter in full battledress, carrying a weapon, and running for his life. We'd need to sprint across the open ground ahead of us, over the junction, not knowing what could be lurking around the corners, before entering, and clearing, the building, all without a hundred bullets ripping my brand-new smock to shreds.

We were joined by another trooper, this one carrying an unloaded Bren. He was relishing in the chaos around him, there was something in his eyes that told me he was enjoying all this, that and the massive grin on his face.

"Would you chaps like some covering fire?" his tone was wholeheartedly sarcastic, the smile never leaving his face as he slammed a magazine into the top of his gun. His mocking upper-class impression was poor, but as he poured a few more rounds out of his Bren, I noticed that his grouping was good.

It was nice, I thought momentarily, to have someone who could still keep their head, and have a laugh when, at the drop of a hat, a tiny copper projectile could shut down your entire body, for good. But, then again, it was entirely possible that he had gone the complete opposite way and been driven totally insane by the environment we'd found ourselves in. The rate at which he was firing at seemed to suggest the latter. He grinned as he ducked behind our sandbag fortress and popped another magazine into the top of the Bren.

Cocking it, he hopped up enthusiastically, poked his eye down the sight, located on the side of the weapon, and placed his finger menacingly over the trigger.

"On your go gents," his tone made it seem more like an order than a friendly encouragement and it didn't leave us with any other choice than to look at each other with petrified eyes, before leaping over our cover and racing to the wall of the house. Our gunner confirmed his own insanity rather quickly as I just made out the wails of, "Fly you fuzzy wuzzy bees! Fly!"

A manic cackle, like a lunatic standing over a body with a meat cleaver, quickly confirmed my suspicions. He had gone insane. But at least he was covering our movements. The short, sharp bursts of his controlled fire echoed from behind me, spurring me on, as some of his rounds appeared to get incredibly close to my vital organs.

The air around me cracked as bullets zipped past, I didn't know from which side they were coming from, until the heavier boom and snap of a higher calibre weapon focussed its attention on the two nutters sprinting across open ground, letting themselves become target practice. I had tried heavy weaponry in training and one of the easiest to use was the machine guns. Especially firing a machine gun at a nice, big target. Particularly a target that got bigger and bigger the closer it got.

Hunched over, my companion and I raced each other to the finish line, hoping more than anything that we weren't tripped up by the lethal confetti scattering itself around us. The Germans must have been giggling with glee at the two, very large, fish, swimming about in the very tiny barrel, as none of their rounds hit their targets at all. Or maybe they were just having fun watching us skip and dance, avoiding the sharpened projectiles like the world's worst game of hopscotch.

My mind raced, if I was to make it to the building, I needed to be quick, get in as soon as possible and clear the building before they could process what was happening. Which way would the door open? Would they have barricaded themselves in to slow down my progress into the building? Or would they just pepper the doorway at the first sign of movement? *If* I made it to the building, would my partner still be with me?

If I looked back and saw him flapping around like a fish out of water, clutching at his insides as they became his outsides, what would I do? Would I wait for someone else to take his place and let the gunner keep pouring fiery bullets down on my men? Or would I just go in on my own and hope for the best?

I'd hoped for the best so far. I'd go with that.

I skidded into the wall, followed closely by a thud and a gasp as my ally crashed into the wall beside me. We ran our eyes over each other as we both checked for any missed wounds, the power of the adrenaline in us made me feel like no pain was possible. No blood from what I could see, he gave me a quick nod which I returned. We'd made it.

My eyes widened as I watched him slowly draw his bayonet, before clicking it into place on the end of his rifle, a grotesque extension of his own arm. I knew how to use them, I'd stuffed them into sacks of straw before, but the thought of plunging it deep inside someone, pushing harder at the indication of resistance, then drawing it out covered in the blood of a human being terrified me. I dressed myself down and prepared myself for what I was about to do. Kill.

I half expected an over exaggerated squeak to come from the door as it pivoted on its hinges, but no such sound came as he silently pushed open the door, before storming in on tip toes, heading for the far corner, trying to dominate the room. I followed close behind, gun raised, ready to return fire as he was peppered with bullets. The red mist would linger for half a second, before being renewed as I received the same good news. I slammed my eyelids shut, forcing myself into darkness and allowing me to refocus my mind.

We stood for a moment in the room, the dull beating of the machine gun upstairs worryingly resembling the thud of boots charging down the stairs. The continued clamour was good, they weren't coming downstairs for us yet.

The room was desolate and empty, apart from a few upturned boxes, littered with playing cards and coffee mugs. The sweet smell of tobacco wafted its way to my nostrils as a pipe lay solemnly on its side, pining for its owner to return. I thought of my Dad. It had been months since I'd smelled the familiar smell of a pipe. It had been months since I'd seen him.

All the while that my gaze was fixated on the pipe, my mind too, was fixated on my Dad. I felt a reassurance as I looked at it, a presence almost, that he was there, on my side. I could see him now, twiddling his pipe in between his fingers as he read the latest news. It had been months since I had seen him, months since I'd heard from him even and yet, I knew exactly what he had been doing in all that time. Precisely, nothing.

Nothing worth mentioning anyway. He was a changed man, a man who spent his whole day with only his thoughts, only moving to get some food or relieve himself. He was locked in his own head. I needed to make sure that I wasn't right now.

It was a small building, I could see the exterior wall to my right, through a kitchen area, with nothing occupying it other than some jerry cans and opened tins of food.

The wooden staircase ran along the back wall of the room, from left to right and was painted with a layer of flaking mud.

It was my turn to take point, my automatic fire would be more useful as we climbed the staircase and came face to face with a platoon of elite German troops. I wondered how helpful thirty-two, nine-millimetre rounds would be here and imagined the spring forcing each one up and into the chamber, quicker than a ray of sunlight.

My boots seemed to smash into the wooden floorboards sending a shriek up the stairs. I held my breath and steadied my aim as I waited for them to appear at the top of the staircase.

No faces peered back at me, so I continued to the next step. It seemed twice as loud as the first, and as the footsteps were repeated behind me, I became convinced we would be dead within a matter of moments.

My breaths were quicker and shallower, my heart beat faster than it ever had done before causing it to ache and send a message to my stomach to release the butterflies. They flew recklessly around my stomach, as though they'd been given free reign. Sweat rolled down my face, the salty solution stinging my eye as it rolled uninvited into my pupil. I was becoming a nervous wreck, a liability.

The throbbing of the machine gun continued to vibrate up through the soles of my shoes as I inched closer and closer to annihilation. The machine gun was acting as a pacemaker on my heart, only risking a beat every time a quick, violent burst was expelled. I choreographed my breathing too, with the sound of machine gun fire.

With a slight creak, a mixture of the weight on the floorboard and the strain on my knee joints, I reached the top of the stairs. I was sweating profusely now, the slimy liquid threatening to force my weapon down to the ground, and my eyes to be drowned in the solution. I gripped my weapon tighter and reshuffled it to make sure it was firmly embedded into my shoulder. I kept it raised and steady, heading for the open door which stood directly in front of me.

My heart seemed to groan as the vomit inside me began to make an attempt to see the outside of a human body.

The room was empty from what I could see, its door hanging helpfully ajar, but that didn't mean I wouldn't have to clear it. I didn't much fancy the idea of someone sneaking up behind me and pumping me full of lead. I felt almost relieved that my companion had a bolt action rifle, hopefully it would give him enough time to realise his mistake if a .303 found itself suddenly embedded in my body.

The slime of my sweat made me slide all over the place, as if my joints had been lubricated a little too much, I needed to get this all over with, and quickly.

On the balls of my feet I burst into the empty room. It was completely barren, not even a single window to let in any light. A few rolled up hay mattresses lay recklessly in one corner of the room, a large steel jug frequented the other corner, the strong stench of urine acted as all the deterrent I needed to leave the room immediately.

While I'd cleared the room, the landing area was being watched over by a bayoneted rifle and as I breathed in his ear, he prepared to move into the next room. We'd need to move quickly now, the door had banged as I'd burst in and, although there was no movement from the next room, we had to assume that a platoon of enemy soldiers had all heard it from the other side of the wall.

My partner was taking a more casual approach,

moving down the landing quickly, he gently pushed the door on the left and sauntered in, swinging his rifle around so as not to catch his bayonet on the door frame. Like a faithful dog, I followed, expecting to see a body overcome with deadly rounds.

Other than an intact but aging window, the room was identical to the last.

We had one room to go. The rattling intensified as we inched closer, and the sound of communicating voices made every inch of me sweat intensely. The rattling sounded like a never-ending tapping on the floor and it began boring itself into my mind. I scraped my forehead rather than wiping it as I prepared for our final assault.

The door was ajar, I moved over to the other side of the door frame like a ghost, trying to peer into the room. I could make out one figure, his face lit up with each burst of the machine gun.

Tap. Tap. Tap.

I could hear at least one other voice, so pushed two fingers up towards my companion. I waited till I thought I saw his head nod in recognition, before I put up three fingers to signal my uncertainty.

He smirked with a slight shake of his head. We'd been fighting blind for most of the evening already.

He signalled back to me to prepare my Sten. It was a gutsy weapon, it regularly jammed but it was easy enough to clear and its design was odd to put it mildly. The magazine leapt from the side of it, a horizontal feed, like a bone that was broken and pushed its way through the skin, it just didn't look right. I leant it over to one side to check that I could see a round glistening back at me. It sat faithfully right where it should, hopefully it would do what I wanted it to do now. It wasn't meant to work like this, but right now, it served a purpose.

I finished caressing my weapon and by the time I looked up, his hand was already raised, slowly counting down.

5…as the tapping finger continued on the other side of the door, I pulled the Sten over into my left hand…

4…The weight of it began to send a shooting pain down my forearm and into my bicep as I held it steady, it seemed to slip in my clammy hand, but its demise was interrupted by the protruding magazine…

3…The incessant tapping of the machine gun stopped, or at least it seemed to slow as we got closer…

2…Voices sparked up on the other side of the door and an excitable movement could be seen through the crack…

1…my hands began to cramp up around the Sten, as I gripped it for dear life, my hands had frozen around it.

Go.

He pushed the door open with such a force that the hinges almost gave way, it smashed into the wall so hard that it began to shut itself again. Before I missed my brief window, I swung my body round in a wide arc, left arm outstretched and released the Sten into the room, making sure it hit the ground with considerable power, while my companion grabbed the door and slammed it back into its frame.

I felt as if I'd lost one of my own limbs. I felt like one of those many at a party, not knowing anyone other than the host, and with no drink in my hand. I had no idea what to do with my own arms, I'd become so used to carrying a weapon, or clutching the controls of a glider that they didn't really feel like my own limbs anymore.

I felt naked, I had nothing to defend myself with if this hadn't worked. I felt vulnerable.

Immediately, the Sten began discharging its rounds, bouncing around in every direction with its recoil making it buck and kick like a rabid donkey. A round cracked into the door frame just above my head, sending a large splinter shooting through the air before clattering on the other side of the landing. I looked across at him as he mimicked a whistle at me. He stood covering the door, ready to dispose of anyone who came charging out, skewering themselves on his bayonet.

A shriek of pain shot out, just as the magazine emptied itself, the Sten giving a fleeting thump as it settled somewhere in the room. We held each other's gaze throughout, ready to react. I was now weapon-less, what lay on the other side of that door was down to him. I just hoped he was fast enough at cocking his weapon.

He obviously had something against doors, or this one in particular rubbed him up the wrong way as he launched himself shoulder first into the door, sending the door straight into the wall, the frame cracking under this unnatural pressure, letting it rebound back at me as I stepped through.

Two bodies lay chaotically on the floor. One lay in a lagoon of oozing scarlet liquid, motionless. The Sten had done its job, three bullets had caught this one man, two in the neck, the third just grazing his eyebrow. He was dead, no doubt about it. I hadn't seen a corpse before now, but I knew instantly he was my first, and I would never forget it. His eyes had already begun to sink into his skull and his mouth hung open limply, a small trickle of blood coming from one corner. Pity and guilt took a hold of me like never before. This was my first victim. He would have been alive if it wasn't for me. He would have had a family, a life to build, hopes and dreams. And it was *me* who had cut that short. No one else.

The second man lay at the foot of the machine gun, writhing in agony. His face was so screwed up with pain I doubted if he knew we were even in the room with him. His teeth were clamped down hard on each other, but no scream came from his mouth.

He managed to control his breathing and spat a globule of saliva out onto the floor while doing so. He clutched at his lower abdomen, blood seeping through the fleshy bandage he had applied to himself. It looked as though he only had half a middle finger, half of it disappearing up inside himself as he desperately tried to plug the leak.

As he opened his eyes, a look of calm passed over him as he stared at the bayonet. It was pressed into his neck gently, enough to leave a small pockmark on his skin but not enough to draw blood. He spoke, but I couldn't make out what he said, but the whimpering told me everything.

"Do it, please, get it over with."

My new sidekick's nose twitched furiously as he debated with himself whether to plunge the cold steel through the artery. The man was bleeding out, that much was obvious, he would be dead in a matter of moments regardless, my second victim of the night. Outside, all was calm, men began to call out to each other and positions consolidated. The machine gun hung pathetically from the window, like a child who couldn't find his mother. Shell casings littered the floor.

The bayonet was gently pressed further into his neck, but he still did not wince, nor plead with us to stop. He clutched at his stomach, keeping a hauntingly calm eye contact with his opponent. With a frustrated roar, the bayonet was lifted from his neck, while he ran out, screaming for a medic.

It was calm again. The silence reappeared, eerily. It was just me and him. I pulled my Sten from the middle of the room, still hot to the touch and pushed another magazine in. I busied myself making sure my weapon was ready, all my pockets secured, and the sweat cleared from my hands. Anything to avoid the dying man. He grunted and, placing the Sten by my side, I knelt down beside him.

I noticed his teeth were slightly stained on one side, a deeper pigment than the rest. He was the pipe smoker, no doubt about it. He would hang it limply from his mouth, while going about his day to day life. Just like dad.

His eyes widened sadly as he begun to cough and splutter, small bubbles of blood began erupting from his mouth, bursting as they hit the surface of my face. Still, he said nothing, but begged me with his eyes to help him, to get him home; he burned his memory into my mind, into my soul. I found myself pushing my hands down hard on top of his, and watched as inevitably, the leak of his vital fluids began seeping through my own fingers.

His eyes filled with tears as his breathing began to quiver. Coughs of blood began interrupting his panting until the pants turned to wheezes. He spat, and I felt his blood splatter on my face, wiping it with my blood-soaked hand only making matters worse, smearing it across my face to fuse with the camo cream. His wheezes began to penetrate my ears and I felt each one as they too, etched themselves into my mind.

I moved my hands and wiped his hair from his forehead and propped his head up on his helmet.

"I'm sorry mate," I found myself jittering, "I'm…I'm really sorry." I could feel a pool of sorrow bubble up in me as I looked at him. I imagined the heartache and despair that his family would no doubt experience at the news of their son's passing. *If* they ever received news of his passing. He would soon become just another casualty of war, another man occupying an unmarked grave that would gain no visitors, his funeral attended only by those who would chuck the dirt on top of him.

He gradually lifted his arms up, as if he was reaching for something, my face perhaps, but with a thud, they collapsed to the floor, as his eyes began to loll to the back of his head.

His legs began to jerk suddenly, and the wheezes turned more to gargles, as if he was drowning. The gargling continued, like a pot of boiling water simmering on a stove, for a few seconds, as did his flailing arms. I rocked backwards and leant on the heels of my feet, I sat there totally helpless. With one final, overexaggerated twitch of the legs, he suddenly lay quite still. It was all over.

I felt almost relieved for him.

His eyes stayed rolled into the back of his head, which made what I was about to do much easier. I began rummaging around in his pockets trying to find anything of use to me; a weapon, intelligence, ammunition, anything.

It's a necessity of war. It had to be done.

I kept telling myself over and over again that I had to do it, I had no other choice. This was war. He was on one side, I on the other. That was just the way things had turned out. In fact, he had been shooting at me not three minutes ago. But I hadn't even offered him the chance of surrender. I had butchered him. I continued to give myself a hard time as I slowly realised that justifying a cold act is more difficult when you're trying to reason with yourself.

His mouth had already locked open, in an agonising scream and I could see that his tongue was already beginning to dry out rapidly. The smell of tobacco still lingered around the opening of his mouth, a stale smell clinging to him, reluctant to give up the final piece of evidence of his existence.

I struggled as I unbuttoned his tunic, my hands shaking in protest at my actions. Parting his tunic with my quaking hands, I saw a small emblem stitched to the inside of his jacket, but it didn't look like a Swastika or even any other German insignia. I yanked it over to one side, so as to catch it in the light of the moon. It was a small red and white crest sewn just by his heart.

He had died for a country that wasn't even his. He was a Pole. I couldn't help but let my mind wander as it tried to make sense of why he was here. I felt sorry for him again as I thought about the brutality of forced conscription, the poor conditions he would have lived in back home and the murder he had already seen. Or maybe he *had* been a diehard Nazi.

I had felt unstoppable, charging across the bridge, armed men on either side of me, charging towards a moral, just war. Now, I felt alone, ashamed and weak, like the slightest breeze would totally overwhelm me.

Regardless of what I told myself he had done, I retrieved the mattress from the other room and rested it over the top of him, as a Bren gun team sauntered in to take advantage of our new vantage point.

"Well done mate," one of them sparked up with a pat and squeeze on the shoulder.

I trudged back outside, dejected.

8

20th November 1917
06.52 hours

THE GROUND almost gave way as I leapt down from the ridge, my knees cracking as my feet smashed into the earth below. Gunfire rattled off just behind me as large chunks of soil were catapulted upwards before crumbling into a fine dust over the ground.

Bullets hissed and cracked as they zipped past my ear, followed by sobering thuds as they pulverised anything in their deadly path. I bent over and charged forwards to make myself a smaller target.

I aimed for the tank, keeping my eyes fixed on her without blinking as my arms pumped my whole body in a surging motion. I kept my eyes fixed firmly on the faded caricature of the duck, watching it bob violently up and down, as if I stood on the deck of a distressed ship. My teeth ached as I clamped them down on one another, and I hissed out of the side of my mouth as I sucked and expelled air as quickly as I could, saliva seeping out of the seal as I pounded my way across the uneven ground.

I felt the revolver make a leap for freedom out of my hand, and a renewed, more intense grasp around the grip of it sent a shooting pain up my arm.

I was a few feet from the tank now, and I chanced a look away from the faded paintworks adorning Doris. I could make out the door opening before the Lieutenant Harper's head peered inquisitively around the side. He looked surprised to hear so much gunfire and chaos, like he had just been rudely awoken while he lay sunbathing on the seafront. He looked even more surprised when the figure charging towards him erupted.

I began launching my arms around like a madman, wildly gesticulating at the Lieutenant.

"Get on the Lewis guns now!" I screamed. My voice was so strained that it pained me as I screeched at him, I could have done with a pint of cold water to soothe my aching vocal chords. Normally, I would have felt hideously ashamed at screaming at my superior, but this time I felt entirely justified, the Lieutenant on the other hand seemed shell shocked for a moment, before ducking back inside.

I reached the tank, but my legs wanted to carry on running, I was going too fast to stop now. I clattered into the side of the tank with a clang, nearly knocking myself out. I had no time to feel and evaluate the pain, so I yanked myself into the relative safety of Doris.

The smoke had cleared from the cabin, and an almost fresh air had replaced it, although the smell of fumes and grease permanently lingered. I snatched my helmet from my seat at the front of the tank and plonked it on with such a force that I gave myself a pounding headache. I sniffed sharply, a futile attempt at gaining some composure, before throwing myself towards my seat in the tank and took up position on the small machine gun that poked bravely from the front.

I forced the revolver down the waistband of my trousers.

There was an eerie calmness inside the tank. Lieutenant Harper had been smoking and a well annotated map lay nonchalantly on top of the engine. The only thing that seemed to be missing from this retreat was the sound of a gramophone scratching as it started up, churning out some of Harper's favoured pieces of music. He knew we couldn't stand it, yet he was an officer, and it was their job to wind us up, and so, his gramophone would take pride of place in his billet, somehow always coming through the action completely unscathed. Rounds hadn't quite started hitting Doris yet, but it wouldn't be long before she was thrust sacrificially in between us and a barrage of bullets once again.

We shook violently as a six-pound round was pushed forcefully down the barrel and I could just make it out as it burst a short distance away. I watched as Bill Ash, a man who I would have deemed too large to squeeze into a steel container, leant forcefully into the aiming rod of the gun, grunting with exertion as it traversed round. The six-pounder was a funny thing, a whacking great gun that took up the majority of the tank, and capable of wreaking death and destruction on so many. But it was operated with a small trigger, a pistol grip that would have looked more at home on Lieutenant Harper's Webley than on a giant ex-naval weapon.

The Lieutenant began firing rounds off to my right, in controlled two round bursts. He caught me looking over at him.

"We don't have much ammo left, maximum damage, minimal rounds," he was cool and level headed, like a serial killer who was used to dismembering bodies at the flick of a trigger. His crystal clear, British accent was frustrating, not a syllable seemed out of place when he spoke. It seemed appropriate though, as he had been allowed to go to Sandhurst early, his father being very high up in the chain of command. He was earmarked for greater things, greater things than perishing in a metal box surrounded by working class oiks that is. He was absolutely determined, committed to fighting his way out of every situation and forcing his way up that ladder if he had to.

He finished off the rounds he had in the Lewis in a prolonged, uninterrupted burst, tapping the Lewis gun affectionately, indicating it was now under my command. I shuffled around the tank, catching my head on one of the protruding steel beams, clanging on my helmet and not helping my headache in the slightest.

I smashed a plate-like drum on top of the Lewis, wiggled it so it fell into place and hammered it down with my fist. Pulling the cocking handle let out a satisfying clunk. As I did so, the recognisable twang of rounds ricocheting off the side of the armour, resounded its ghostly toll.

I followed his command to the letter, aiming vaguely at the dark mass that seemed to be moving up ahead, the ball mechanism squeaking gently as I manoeuvred the weapon around.

"Where are the others?!" came a shriek, and I felt my finger twitch on the trigger, startled. My heart fell to my knees, I'd forgotten about them.

"Somewhere up on the ledge there, where that front rank is now!" I'd charged so hard, focused so desperately on the caricature, that I had neglected to look behind to check on the progress of my other three crewmates. There wouldn't have been much I could have done, armed only with a puny revolver, but I felt responsible regardless.

"And Jack?!"

The following silence was all we had needed to hear. In the space of five minutes we had lost half of our crew, including our most experienced mechanic and, our best chance of getting out of here with Doris.

"They're gone then, forget about them," the Lieutenant was getting colder by the second. I suddenly lost all sense of guilt and was intensely happy that I was on the inside of this tank, with the Lieutenant, and not left on the outside. But then again, I was on the inside with Harper and I wondered how long it would be before he shot me and himself to stop us being captured.

"Eric, get up on the six-pounder, get everything out," he seemed to barely raise his voice, it was almost inaudible above the harshness of the clamour around us. Rounds tinkled delicately on the floor as they spat their way out of the breech, as rounds thumped into the armour that was protecting us.

What he had been doing before I didn't know, but our second mechanic, Eric, instantly leapt up, with a renewed sense of purpose, and positioned himself behind the gun. I could see him struggle out of my periphery as he heaved a round up and into the breech.

Bill let out another round, and an odd tinging filled my eardrums as he opened up the breech, a red-hot case clattering to the floor. Suddenly Bill shrieked, and he flew backwards, colliding with the back of the sponson which he occupied. I heaved my way over to him, steadying myself on the beams and rivets around me. The heat of the engine still emanated defiantly from the centre of the tank, even though it had been unused for a while now.

"Get the breech shut!" Bill screamed at me as he lay spread out, completely incapacitated. I slammed it shut as I heard more rounds hurtling up the barrel of the gun, as the volume of bullets from outside intensified greatly. Bill was already losing a great amount of blood, and, as he clutched his shoulder, he gave me a grunt of encouragement to get back to the Lewis. His hands had already been stained scarlet by the waterfall that now began to trickle down his tunic. His body shook as he began to cough up more blood than I had ever seen before, as if he was violently retching and trying to be sick. The blood began dribbling down his body and began convening, unceremoniously on the floor of the tank.

"Go," he hissed at me as I stood staring at the gaping wound in his shoulder. I gripped his arm with enthusiasm before turning my back on him and heading to the front of the tank.

I felt good as I pulled the Lewis gun out of its slumber and just as I ran out of rounds, Eric released a deadly dart. The whole world seemed to lurch backwards as it was expelled, throwing me off my footing and sending my knee plummeting into the concrete-like steel below.

I picked up another dish and used all my energy to push myself back up to standing. I let my leg hover momentarily, as I reloaded, trying to rest it before sending shockwaves back up my leg when the pressure of body-weight was reapplied.

Wincing slightly, I took a wider stance as I fired off a few more rounds, preparing myself for the next earthquake in little Doris. The Lewis gun kicked and bucked in my hands, my left hand attempting to steady the rabid wolf as it threw itself around. A rush of air flicked my protruding hair about as it tried to suck in oxygen and the moving parts caused a slight breeze.

The rounds intensified as I began to see more figures appearing from the woods. They had changed movements, they weren't coming down the track anymore, they had spread out into the woods and were flanking us. They continued to move as one, like a wave, stubbornly continuing towards the shore. As quickly as one man fell, and a gap opened up, it would be replaced by another slate grey uniform, identical to the last.

"Bill's dead!" came the cry, but I had no option but to ignore it, and keep the pressure on the sea of grey ahead of me. I didn't have the opportunity to work out who had screamed it, it could have even been a German voice for all I knew, I just kept my finger depressed on the trigger.

We were dangerously low on ammunition. I had one full magazine left before the Lewis became obsolete. I could see three rounds for the six-pounder. Soon we would be without ammunition and surrounded.

My mind briefly flicked to what would happen. There were only two outcomes to this situation right now. We died, which I didn't much fancy. Or we surrendered. And surrender simply wasn't an option for us anymore. We'd come too far.

To my right I heard the Lieutenant curse as he threw his Lewis upwards, giving up the protection of our flank, letting it dangle limply out of its peephole.

"I'm out!" he exclaimed in total frustration, the first time he had raised his voice so far.

I kept my Lewis buried into my shoulder, letting it abuse me and bully my joints. Rounds trickled on the floor repetitively and the smell of cordite hung in the stagnant air.

I was beginning to make out facial features and individual characteristics as I ran out of ammo. Eric fired off the last of his rounds. Letting go of the Lewis, I pulled sharply on the two levers that operated the steel flaps, I wanted to make sure they were firmly closed.

"That's it then," Eric piped up.

"Let's try and get this thing moving, shall we?" said Lieutenant Harper, I couldn't knock him for his fierce determination, he desperately wanted to climb that ladder of promotion. The fact of the matter however was this, we needed a total crew of eight to drive this beast, four of us needed just to get the engine going, and, the last time I had checked, only four of us now occupied this particular tank, and one of them was dead.

Loyally, Eric heaved at the engine as we took up position at the front, in our unpadded and uncomfortable seats. It was nice to take some weight off my knee for a moment though.

The engine spluttered into life, before weakly giving up seconds later, blessing us all with an upheaval of emotions.

I felt sick to the very pit of my stomach as the rounds that Doris had so valiantly repelled for so long began to subside. Subside into a silence.

We sat there panting, as I shut my eyes and let the sting of the grease run its course. I thought of home. My wife, who I had barely seen since we were married, would soon forget me, forget my face, as I became another life lost in France. She would soon be widowed, at such a young age too. I'm sure tears would have formed in my eyes, had they not felt so dry and irritable.

The crack of a revolver forced my eyes open.

"We take as many with us as possible." I briefly amused myself with the idea that slogan lessons were taught in the first week at Sandhurst, as almost all the officers I'd met seemed to have a catchphrase for every occasion.

I shifted my weight over to one side as I retrieved the revolver from my waistband. His blind patriotism and warrior like determination was draining yet inspiring. The revolver was cold, a blessed relief to the clammy and dampened hands that it was welcomed by. My hands slipped over the grip as I caressed its every groove.

The sound of my heart, thumping in my ears, began to subside, as the effects of the adrenaline began to pass, a paralysing sense of fear now caught up with me. I began to notice all the aches and pains that emitted from every part of my body, and it became more and more of a struggle to ignore them.

Wiping my hands on my trousers, I took up position under a cover, designed to fire through when the enemy clambered on top, as did Eric. The Lieutenant camped out by the door.

I pulled my tunic off, wanting to be comfortable when I died at the very least. I settled down into a perch, directly underneath, ready to jump up and flick open the hatch, surprising all of our uninvited guests. My knee was in total agony, a piercing pain shooting up my thigh. My mouth was bone dry and a tiny wheeze was escaping from my mouth with every breath. There was a calmness about me though. One that I had not experienced before. I was accepting that I was minutes from death.

I wiped the greasy hair that clung to my forehead with the back of my hand, a layer of dirt and grime attaching itself as I did so.

The ticking of the Lieutenant's watch and the ringing in my ears was slowly replaced with harsh whispers. I was surprised we could hear them at first, but that surprise was quickly replaced by a paralysing fear, a terrifying realisation of death.

They knew we were in here. No ammo. Low on energy. Low on fighting spirit.

I imagined God watching the scene unfold before him. A group of German soldiers all surrounding Doris, notches and blemishes all over her from the punishments of angry ammunition. Their weapons raised in anticipation of the enemy hopping out in surrender, all slightly too young and too nervy around the trigger area of their rifles. The growling officer would smugly march us off into captivity or leave us in a ditch with a crater in the back of our skulls for taking so many of his men. The scene unfolding before God would be catastrophic, waiting for the right time to pull me off His earth, leaving a trail of utter devastation behind.

9

6th June 1944
00.22 hours

A SILENCE ENGULFED us once again. A moment of almost disbelief. We had done it; the bridge was ours.

I stood outside, propped up on the front door, with my clearing partner by my side.

For another soldier, this would have been a moment of triumph, a time to relish in, to refine my storytelling in preparation for the years of dinner parties after the war. But the incessant tapping of the machine gun was still rattling around the inside of my head, showing no signs of stopping, not even to reload.

Tap. Tap. Tap.

The immortal scream of the Pole echoed around my empty mind at intervals, halting any sense of jubilation or pride.

"Len, by the way," he muttered, as he thrust a cigarette packet under my nose. He had no facial features, none of them did, they had all disappeared under layer upon layer of face cream, it was almost a competition to see who could pack the most on. His face looked muddied and filthy, just the way he would have wanted it, but his eyes burned brightly against the dark pigment.

"I was in stick number one, what about you?" He gave the cigarette packet a little shake. I could have died alongside this bloke, and yet I hadn't even known his name.

I pursed my lips as if I was going to answer but hesitated. Obliging, I pinched at a cigarette with bloodied fingernails. They had browned slightly, but some of the dirt began to rub itself into the cigarette as I twirled it in between my fingers, inspecting them.

The cigarette shook gently in my hands as a quiver slowly took hold.

"Here," he muttered again before dousing my hands in water from his canteen before mimicking the motion of wiping them down my legs.

Again, I silently obliged, before taking his offer of a light. The familiar smell of smoke calmed me, sending me to a place far from where I was standing. The first time I had smelled smoke was at school, the changing rooms to be precise, after my first attempt at playing rugby.

"You're good Chambers," he grunted, "a natural talent." I could only nod my approval at the sports teacher, I was bewildered by his apparent compliment. A few minutes later and he was belting me once again for disobedience, his favourite method of "building character."

Men smoked, a couple spoke to a local who had appeared like a meerkat, wanting to get a peek at the liberation. He staggered around, embracing and cheering as many of his liberators as he could, his face smattered with ample face cream by the time he had finished. Some busied themselves by retrieving ammunition, fixing radios or requisitioning enemy weapons. A couple even dished out a few bars of chocolate liberated from a dead German's pack.

I turned down the offer of chocolate. I felt uneasy. I had helped kill a man, I had taken a life. I had become a murderer. We were no better than them, they killed, but we killed, I hadn't even offered him the chance to surrender.

I pushed my index finger into my breast pocket, and felt for my chocolate bar I kept stashed away. Its solid form comforted me as I withdrew.

"You're one of our glider boys, right?" He didn't wait for a reply, but began thanking me and the other lads in the regiment for getting them down safely and calmly. He didn't know the half of it.

Letting out my last puff of smoke with an exaggerated sigh, I flicked it across the dirt track and rubbed my face. I had only experienced a few minutes of combat and already I felt battle hardened. Although, I couldn't tell the difference between being battle hardened and downright scared.

Len could sense my apprehension. For some reason he had adopted me, he had seen a necessity to take me under his wing and guide me in my first experience of war. He was young, I supposed all of us were, but he struck me as one who had been in battle before. He seemed like he knew exactly the kind of thing he'd have to deal with, and he seemed able to cut away from what had just happened and carry on talking about his girlfriend.

People were always taking me under their wing, especially from day one in the army. During training for the invasion, one particular man, Company Sergeant-Major Baker, had stuck in my mind. He seemed like a kindly fellow, always keeping a watchful eye over training, and making a point of asking individuals how they were. I knew it was something he had been told to curtail, but it seemed inherent in him, like he simply couldn't stop. As I thought of him, I wondered what he was doing tonight, surely he was part of this Op, possibly in the second wave, but he would be involved somewhere along the line, most people I met were in some way.

"Come on mate, let's hop to it." I couldn't for the life of me place his accent. One moment he was Home Counties, next he was a broad Brummie, but then he had sounded like a boy from the Valleys. I made a mental note to ask him, as soon as I felt ready to talk again.

We occupied ourselves by replacing sandbags, building a mini fortress around an anti-aircraft gun and machine gun so it faced back towards the village, in the inevitable act of defending a counter attack.

"…you got a girlfriend mate?"

"Yeah…" I croaked, only just having time to clear my throat before Len was off again.

"Good for you. Good for you. Of course, we have only…"

I laid my Sten against the steel beam of the bridge, checking on it regularly as if it were a new-born baby in the night.

"…and so, I suppose I talk rather a lot when I'm nervous. But then again…"

He continued jabbering on about his life at home, his girlfriend, his old job, what he would do when he got back, anything just to keep his jaw moving it seemed. I didn't take the blindest bit of notice, maybe I should have, he probably mentioned where he was from. My mind was elsewhere, it was still with the Pole, lying under the straw mattress until some other poor soul was tasked with the job of burying him. Maybe he wouldn't be buried at all. I supposed by morning it was possible that the whole village would be flattened, and we would all be buried under layer upon layer of rubble.

"…and so, I decided to volunteer, rather than wait for the call-up. According to my brother you get a rough deal if you wait for the draft, he joined up back in thirty-nine when…"

I watched intently as the moonlight glistened on the river, illuminating the banks on either side. It was perfectly flat, completely still, not a single ripple was to be seen. It was like a perfect sheet of glass, mirroring the sky with pinpoint accuracy, every star that adorned the sky, so too it was on the water. If it wasn't for the freezing temperature, I would have been half tempted to go in for a dip. I decided to wait and see what the weather was like in the morning.

In another lifetime I could have taken a longboat along it and taken in the French countryside. I would have basked in the warm sunshine as it kissed my face, letting a few freckles poke out from the depths of my skin. Maybe in another lifetime I would have sailed underneath it in the summer sunshine, instead of being on it in the middle of the night.

Len's blabbering suddenly stopped. I hadn't paid attention, but the continuous soundtrack had become almost soothing to me, knowing that with everything going on in my mind, someone was able to carry on as normal. It had become my anchor.

The continuous absence of his voice seemed to continue for a few moments longer. I turned to see what had made him stop, half expecting to see an officer standing there ready to bark at us, or maybe even the Prime Minister congratulating us on a cracking job well done. I would shake his hand enthusiastically, after double checking the hygiene standard of my own, before smiling broadly for the cameraman stood by his side. The pin stripes of his suit would look ridiculous amongst all the sea of khaki that was running around us, causing a clamour as they all fought for a glance. I would tell him how much I had enjoyed taking the fight to the enemy, making them run scared as if Death himself was chasing them, scythe drawn and all.

But I was wrong.

Len's face was pressed against the hard steel structure of the bridge, almost kissing the tip of my boots, with his arms stretched out like a child pretending to be a plane. His rifle lay by his side, knocked over as he collapsed into the wall of sandbags it was propped up against. A few of the sandbags hung precariously over the edge of the wall as he'd clattered into them, dragging them downwards.

The back of his helmet had a gaping hole. The netting over it was twisted and entangled in the cave that had burrowed through his helmet. There was no blood, just a dark abyss, a ravine of unknown depth tunnelling its way into his skull. It reminded me almost of an entrance to a rabbit warren, a fairly humble entrance, but the extent to which the rabbit had excavated, completely hidden.

I couldn't make out a speck of blood on him. No hint of it on his kit or his uniform, and his helmet was in almost pristine condition. Gravity beckoning it to the floor, some of Len's blood began to trickle its way down the back of *my* neck, a place on the ground already earmarked for its landing zone by a pathfinder force of blood.

I interrupted the flow of the stream as I stuck my hand below the line of the back of my helmet. Slowly wiping my clammy, numb hand around my neck, I felt it collect a sample of Len's scarlet fluid.

I inspected my hand again, I was shaking this time, and watched as the moon lit up every detail of my hand. Parts of it were unaffected, tiny diamonds of sweat glinting in the light of the midnight moon. Great smears of blood soiled the rest, burying itself into every line and crevice in my hand. For the second time in the space of an hour I found myself inspecting a dead man's blood on my hands.

It was a deep red, darker than any other blood I had ever seen before, it almost didn't look like blood.

I blinked furiously as I fought back tears, a mixture of strenuous breathing through my nose and violent intakes of breath through my mouth followed. The world around me swayed as the nausea kicked in and, for a moment, it felt as though the bridge had been blown and I stood on thin air, waiting for the moment I was sent plummeting into the freezing waters below.

I tried to compose myself as best I could, while I stared at Len's corpse. I willed him to talk, to say anything, more for my own sake rather than for his. I needed that new-found normality back. I felt sick force its way through my stomach and attempt to get out. My stomach clamped as I began to retch while an agonising fire raged within me. I bent over, trying to force it out of the pits of my belly, but before I could, I felt myself clatter into the floor.

I waited for the explosion of pain I suspected that would follow being hit by a German round. But none of it came, it was almost as if I was suddenly at peace with everything that had happened.

The vomit had vanished, the hyperventilating had ceased. I couldn't feel my hands shaking anymore, instead, I lay perfectly still. There was no pain, no feeling of impending doom or dread, just a brief moment of serenity. Was this death? Had I passed over? Who would I meet?

I wasn't in heaven that was for sure. The vomit had returned and pushed itself out more forcefully, leaving an incredible taste in my mouth and a burning sensation in my nose.

I spat out a rather pathetic attempt at vomiting as noises began reaching my ears again. Another confirmation that I wasn't in heaven. Screams and gunshots rang out, before a hissing reached my ear with an accompanying lump of weight. I was almost disappointed that I wasn't dead, I certainly wasn't relieved to find myself still in the hellhole of France.

"When you hear 'sniper', you get down you idiot!" The hiss was so threatening it could have been an enemy soldier, the tone of murderous aggression was unbelievable. Lying on me silently for a moment too long, I felt like a child as the weight removed itself from me. Vulnerable. Only still living and breathing because I had always seemed to be someone else's responsibility. Sergeant-Major Baker's, Charlie's, Len's and now my hissing helper. I wanted to curl myself up and tuck myself behind the sandbags until I felt I could come out again.

I clung to my knees in desperation as I huddled myself into the sandbags, letting them engulf me. I stared at the bridge, great beads of blood had begun trickling down, racing each other to the floor. Some droplets were interrupted by the random bits of brain matter decorating the bridge, bits of Len, ingrained into the bridge forever.

It would be wiped clean soon enough, a light rainfall would be all that it needed. It would probably be reopened as a bridge before too long and years later, car after car will trundle over it not knowing that men had become part of this bridge. They would all be forgotten.

A fury rose up inside me, an aggression and hatred so strong for the generation not yet born that I leapt up, and following the red-hot tracer rounds that pierced the chill of the night, emptied a magazine into the French air. They were just token rounds, there was no way they would even get close to the sniper. But it made me feel good. It made me feel like I had taken revenge.

Len hadn't known what had happened to him. It was easier for me to take knowing that one moment, he was talking about the comforts he had in his life; his home, his girlfriend, his family and the next, he was just gone. He didn't exist anymore.

I shook my arm out to relieve it from the pummelling it had just taken from the Sten. It hurt more than normal, just standing there I could almost feel the bruising form around my joints. I pulled another magazine from my belt and as I did so watched carefully as one man stepped up with a PIAT gun.

It was a burdensome weapon, but one that was deadly

if used correctly. I watched as he was almost propelled to the other side of the bridge as he pulled the trigger, forcing a spear tipped projectile out of the end. It was lobbed through the air, and came down with such a crash on a nearby building I felt the ground quiver slightly, maybe it was as scared as I was.

The round had fallen short, but the man's determination was to be commended. Rounds kept pinging their way towards the building the sniper was in before the anti-aircraft gun ripped rounds through the walls. The low, booming, tapping noise was far more comforting to me than the constant tapping of the German machine gun. It probably had something to do with the fact that these rounds were directed away from me, not trying to cut me down. Sparks lit up as they pummelled their way into the brickwork, before large chunks of the wall began flying out in all directions. A short burst, and most of the side of the building was gone.

A few overenthusiastic men charged up to the building, weapons at the ready. Silence ensued once more, an uneasy perfection had engulfed us.

Men began to mill around once more, lighting cigarettes and restarting conversations with one another, all the while the water remained like glass, faithfully reflecting the moonlight. I was alone this time, no one to help me clean my hands, no one to offer me a cigarette or restart a conversation with. All these men around me, and I felt alone, totally abandoned.

The whole episode can't have taken longer than twenty seconds. The men seemed more focused this time, they didn't cheer or celebrate, they worked in pairs, one of them weapon drawn, eyes peeled.

The anger had left me in that short burst of rounds. I was already on my way to forgetting about Len.

His body was being dragged back towards the landing zone, where a khaki blanket would be pulled up over him, waiting in the grotesque queue, along with the Pole, to be buried.

10

20th November 1917
07.04 hours

THE GERMANS' sick game of hide and seek continued as they staggered closer and closer to our Doris. Doris was dead, so were most of her crew, the last three perched inside, ready for the same fate.

Bill had begun to let out a putrid stink, exaggerated by the heat and enclosed situation we found ourselves in. Lieutenant Harper had pulled his tunic over Bill, so we didn't have to feel his eyes critiquing our last few moments. Even with just the three of us inside, with the engines off, the atmosphere had become suffocating. I was desperate to open up the hatch in front of me and suck in fresh, clean air and feel it cleanse my insides as it swirled its way around. The face of the German on the other side played on my mind, so much so that I had to settle for the imaginative air that I had convinced myself of.

Eric had begun whispering to himself, a prayer of some kind, or a plea. His muttering had intensified and in the absence of all other sound it seemed as if he was screaming, his murmuring sliding its way around the cab only interrupted by another sentence of madman rambling.

I didn't know too much about him. I knew he was Welsh and that he had volunteered rather than wait to be conscripted. Fair enough, I had done the same. He was quiet, and kept himself to himself, never socialising with the rest of the crew on the outside, always taking himself off somewhere before miraculously reappearing just as we had orders to move off. Whether a man was loud or quiet was neither here nor there, for, in a tank, everything was done by hand signals anyway. It seemed to suit him.

From looking at him though, he had had a tough upbringing. His eyes seemed to display a maturity that the rest of him hadn't quite caught up with yet, the kind when a young man has seen a horrific scene before him, understanding the true nature of man. They burned a deep blue, a penetrating blue, but also held a sorrowful glare behind them. His eyes troubled me, they would stay with me for the rest of my life.

I had wondered for hours about what had caused him the pain and sorrow that he didn't express, the tragedy or the trauma that had shaped the man he was today. Maybe it had been this very war. It was entirely possible that before this war had started, he had been bright eyed and endlessly happy, but now his eyes were full of pure anguish. The death and the callousness of the human heart was enough to make anyone emotionless, given away only by the mournful tone of the pupils. Maybe he could tell the same of me. I hadn't looked in a mirror for what felt like years so had no idea of how my facial features gave away my past experiences. I had no recollection of how I even looked.

I hoped, at least, that my eyes hid some of the tumultuous thoughts from within. I had started this war as a young patriot, the belief that what I was doing was for my country, to fight for freedom and prosperity. That had soon changed when I saw the power of a six-pounder. A solitary young man, exploding in all directions and scattering himself afar. My eyes seemed torn at what to look at, I could almost feel them separate as one followed his lower leg, while the other followed his head, going in the opposite direction. In the actual event, however, my eyes had fixed firmly on the place where he had once stood, now a smoking, empty crater of mud, no sign of its previous living occupant. This had changed me. I had started this war as a scared patriot, I believed that the enemy had been the antichrist, the very Satan that I had been brought up to pray against, manifested in humanness. We had been told they were all battle hardened, merciless, murderers. But he had been a small boy. I often dreamt of the fear on his face as the shot was ordered, and watched as the shell landed somewhere around his feet, closing his eyes and welcoming death in a reluctant embrace.

Since that moment, I possessed a feeling of regret at every round that was spat out of my Lewis gun, every shell that pummelled its way from Doris. My feelings could not overhang my actions, there would be seven other witnesses to my cowardice, seven others willing to stick a bullet in my skull for not doing my duty. I feared every moment that my cowardice would be seen the moment someone made eye contact, and I desperately hoped my pupils masked the fear, the sorrow that encompassed me.

As I reflected on my own situation, I stroked gently over the oily stubble that had sprouted from my chin. The scratching noise that it produced echoed off the steel structure and shocked me into submission.

I distracted myself by looking over at Eric once more. I noticed for the first time that his hands were tough, covered in a layer of grime and grease. They were larger than how I imagined they should have been and they were dry and cracked. He must have lost some sort of feeling in them as on more than one occasion he had placed his hand on the searingly hot engine, as it was glowing red hot, for a number of seconds before calmly removing it.

He used to wear a ring. I thought at first it was a wedding ring, but then discarded this thought on account of his young age. But then again, we were all young men, in age at least, but the experience of war had only served to mature us, to age us. He hadn't made mention of a wife or a girlfriend, always pushing the subject matter away at any given opportunity, focusing instead on Doris or the war itself.

Maybe he had been married to Doris, as a mechanic, he knew her better than any of us, and encouraged her in helping us out of tricky situations. We had all been married to Doris, in one way or another. She had given us all the emotions of love, nervousness, excitement and stability, when we had first seen her. It was exactly the same feeling that I had experienced when I met Mary. It was a chance meeting, although I knew her from the village, I had never actually spoken to her. She never came into the bakery until her mother fell desperately ill. I often told myself at the time that her mother becoming gravely ill was possibly the best thing that ever happened in my life. I never, however much I wanted to, told her that that was how I had felt about her mother, as she would die a few weeks after we had been married. It seemed easier to fall in love back then, there was no war, no daily demonstrations of different ways to die or watching men butcher each other. But then, there was a war, and I took the King's shilling. I took one step closer to death that day and, deep down, I knew it. I married Mary on my first leave home. If I was to die, I wanted her to benefit from it. My feelings for Mary, in her absence in my life, had grown, likewise my feelings for Doris, in her constant presence, had continued to grow right up to this moment, where all I wanted was to be as far away from the steel box as I could be.

I thought of Thetford forest again, the constant singing of the birds would be enough to keep my soul content. Mary would often sit there with me for hours, her eyes tightly shut, letting the soundtrack enter her, with no need for the landscape to play its part. She would often escape to a different world in her mind. A world that I could never see.

Eric wasn't wearing the ring today. It was noticeably absent, as he had always kept it brilliantly clean so that, even when his hands were filthy, a dull sparkle would still glisten in the light.

There was no sparkle today, it had gone out.

I wondered what they would do to us, the Germans, if we made it that far. The callousness in the Lieutenant's voice had made me fear him more than them, and I was willing to take my chances in surrendering.

I could imagine us, paraded in front of a garrison of troops, Doris towed behind, the bounty of their expedition displayed for all to see. Each and every one of the young men would have a story to tell when they got back to camp about how they captured a British tank and her crew. No doubt the stories would be embellished and polished up in preparation for their arrival back home. Many hundreds of women would be serenaded with the tale of their bravery and gallantry as they stormed the most heavily armoured weapon of the war. They would be hailed as heroes. We would be muck.

I became more agitated as I came to the realisation that our fate was unknown, and this was more daunting a thought than knowing for sure we were dead. We could be left, face down in the sodden ground of France, forgotten, only to be found in part by an overenthusiastic dog in years to come. I didn't much fancy the idea of a dog parading around with one of my femur in his mouth, dropping it at the feet of his owner. I didn't much like the idea of dying at all.

Besides, I had Mary to get home to. When I was sent to hell, she was all I could think about; my wife, my *new* wife, waiting for me at the door when I got home. Now, she was more of a distant memory than a wife, a photograph pinned carefully to the ceiling of Doris. She peered out from the sepia stained card, an expression of hope, but anxiety, all masked by a sweet smile that poked out from under her top lip. Unpicking it from its resting place, above my driving seat, I found myself running my muddied thumb over the surface of the picture, marvelling at the smoothness of her skin. I gave it a quick kiss, and placed it in the breast pocket of my shirt. They could take my life if they wanted, but I didn't want them taking the only picture of my wife that I owned. That would eternally be mine.

I thought about her for a few moments more as I longed to be transported to somewhere in the world that was safe, and to hold her in my arms. She was smaller than me, and it felt good to be able to encompass her whole body in the reach of my arms, like I was able to protect her from an autumnal storm. I missed her smell, I missed the sound of her voice, I missed—

The blunt interruption of heavy, leather boots, clashing between the cold, armoured steel, brought my train of thought to a very abrupt conclusion.

The mutterings inside diminished rapidly, they became echoes in my mind, there to haunt me forever, just like everything else. The voices outside took over and became more excited and jittery as they heaved each other up. I traced their footsteps with my eyes as they began pacing themselves all over Doris. It was now that I realised how thin the armour really was. It was able to stop bullets, most of the time, but the clarity with which I could hear voices and footsteps alarmed me.

Maybe they weren't even going to look in, maybe this was the only trophy they needed. I knew they would, I knew first-hand the sense of power and invincibility one got from standing on a tank, and their confidence would lead to them comfortably coming inside. My heart pounded, threatening to burst out of my chest once more as I worked myself up about the possibility of living and seeing my wife again.

My ears throbbed, as my eyes met Eric's as he looked up from his prayer. His facial expression had changed. It was no longer one of fear and fright but of passion and determination. His eyes had changed too, they no longer spoke of a desolate despair and mournfulness, but of excitement as they zipped from side to side, as if everything that he was seeing was for the first time. He shifted energetically as he moved his hand silently to slide open one of the peep holes.

He looked across to the Lieutenant for his approval.

"Choose your moment," he said with his eyes. Eric obliged, holding his position like a demented human statue, before reaching down again and inspecting his weapon. I could see from where I was perched that he had a full complement of brass rounds waiting patiently in his revolver. He clicked the cylinder so it lined up perfectly with the rest of the weapon. I hoped desperately that six rounds would be all he needed to rid us of the Germans that were now surrounding us.

The click was so startling it felt as if everything had stopped for Eric.

He glanced across at Lieutenant Harper and nodded, who gave a slight nod in return. He stood on the balls of his feet, bouncing around as if some demon was possessing him, but also slightly hunched over, his knees bent to get a good angle. He looked like a Jack in the box that had been wound up hours ago, without the final crank of the handle.

Slowly, he turned his head to face me. A smirk had formed on his face and as he nodded at me, he knew exactly what was about to happen. He was pumped up. He was so full of adrenaline and excitement that all sense of danger and perspective had clearly deserted him. I was slightly less confident in his actions, he was about to get us killed, no doubt about it.

Revolver in his right hand, he raised it, barrel pointing straight up and bought it up to about shoulder height. I could just see him line the fixed blade at the end of the weapon with the notch at the rear, slightly closing his left eye as he did so. With his left hand, he deliberately moved for the latch on the hole. With one swift flick of the wrist, he snapped it open.

A pause developed. It was as if Eric had opened the hatch to some children, playing joyfully on the tank, no care in the world about the war that enraged around them. Either that or there was more that he could see than we had expected. His face showed no signs of changing, he knew he was committed now. But whatever it was out there, it wasn't children.

The pause was mutual, the Germans hadn't fired a shot, not even a raised voice. Maybe they had been complacent, maybe they thought we had all been killed already. Or perhaps they were waiting for a small stick, a whiteish hanky tied to it in surrender. That would have been my expectation. The pause went on for too long, with Eric's action only confirming our fates. Maybe we could have lived if he hadn't given the game away.

The grotesque game of hide and seek was over, they had found us. There was no reciprocal round of this hide and seek, there was only one ending. Death. A twisted end to a harmless game.

Eric's smirk was permanently stained on his face as he managed to fire off three rounds before I heard a heavy thump on the steel as a body collapsed and rolled its way down to the ground. Shouts leapt up from outside the tank, angry, aggressive shouts. The Lieutenant and I could do nothing other than sit and watch, and hope it would all end peacefully.

I could smell smoke, amongst the cordite, grease and death, the distinctive smell of cigarette smoke wafted its way through the opening. They *had* been complacent. I looked across at the Lieutenant, his revolver stared back at me, but his eyes were fixed obsessively on Eric. He was crouched down now, ready to step over the body of Eric and take his place, as he inevitably fell.

Three rounds was all Eric managed though, as a volley of bullets began thumping their way into Doris as Eric was catapulted to the ground by a lucky round that made its way through the opening. Rounds continued peppering in and around the hole, great twangs hopping around the inside, and the outside of Doris. I prayed for a ricochet or two that might fool them into thinking we were fighting back, and give us a stay of execution.

If anything, the rounds intensified. I felt as if a great, cast iron bucket had been placed over my head, while a hundred people threw pebbles and shook me within an inch of my life.

He lay on the floor of the tank, weapon raised in his right hand still, as his left clamped around the wound that had opened up on his upper arm. I peered curiously as I could see the individual layers of muscle, bright pink, protruding from under his fingers. Blood quickly seeped through the inadequate seal provided by his hand and the colour drained from the rest of his body. He paused as he took in the sudden change in circumstances.

I sensed the Lieutenant begin to move as he went to cover our opening. As he did so, I heard a number of boots leap off the tank, crunching their way round to the door. I turned, revolver slipping in my hand as I raised it to the hatch.

I glanced at Eric as the smirk quickly ran away from his face. His face had started to look clammy and ashen. His grip loosened on his wound and he let his left-hand fall to the floor. Blood ran from his hand as if the wound itself was on it, pooling into a small puddle rapidly. Slowly, he lowered his right arm, letting the revolver clatter to the ground, joining his arms.

He joined the rest of us, resigned to defeat, whatever form that defeat would come in. It didn't take long for my question to be answered.

The Lieutenant stood straddling Eric, defiantly staring out of the hole, without his weapon raised. As he stood there a long rod poked its way through the peep hole, only stopping once a gloved hand reached the entrance to the hole. They obviously weren't too interested in keeping prisoners or having a trophy. Maybe they weren't as young as we had anticipated. Perhaps they were hardened veterans of this war, all emotions linked to compassion and sympathy wiped from their minds.

We had just annihilated quite a few of their comrades. Three of us. We had piles of bodies lying outside, families now without brothers, sons, fathers, all of them plucked viciously from the world at a swift tug of a steel trigger. All callously decimated into fleshy confetti by a six-pound brass heavyweight as it slammed into the ground.

Maybe we deserved what was about to come to us. I felt hard done by all the same, we were only following orders, acting on inhibitions fuelled by propaganda from above. I let out a sigh as what felt like minutes ticked by, the deathly rod teasing us as it hung there, above Lieutenant Richard Harper. The rattling at the door subsided and Eric's wheezing as he struggled for breath was the only sound that I could focus on now.

As a faint hiss sparked up, I turned my body and pressed my face into the cooling steel wall, throwing my arms around my side and closed myself off from the rest of the tank. I braced myself for the end, trying to limit the pain I would feel in some small way.

The hiss grew louder and as a more ferocious growl bellowed, it was Eric's scream of agony that I heard first, unintelligible curse words howling from his mouth. The low growl continued, the searing heat quickly reaching me as the tank rapidly became like a perverted kettle. I wanted desperately to turn and observe what was happening, wanting to aid my comrades as they died.

I resisted and, clenching my eyes, I braced myself for the incredible pain that was to come.

11

6th June 1944
01.32 hours

HIS STORY HAD ENDED THERE. He had nothing more to tell me. In between the weeping sobs I could make out the names of men who he had crewed with, men he had lived with, but they were no longer men, just mere memories.

I would never know if he had been the only survivor. I would never know how he made it out of that tank alive. My father had told all of his story that he could. What I did know, is that, in amongst the great gulps for air that he took, a few words snuck from his mouth, as if they'd disobeyed an order to stay inside his head.

"They aren't all evil, Johnny."

As my mother began hurrying into the room, my memory began to fade, and I was brought back to the present, the sound of her feet shuffling on the floorboards, replaced by the sounds of men waiting to die. I couldn't help but think of my situation. I had seen men killed, decimated, transformed beyond all recognition in the name of what? A war to end all wars? My father's war would end nothing, neither would mine, in fact it would probably just fuel wars for years to come.

The unborn generation, the generation I had directed so much anger and hatred towards before, now got my wholehearted compassion. They hadn't seen their first daylight yet and it had already been decided that it would be them who fought in the next war. They would fight against larger armies, weapons more powerful and more destructive than the ones that went before, and they would undoubtedly experience death on a much larger scale than ever before.

I wondered what I would look like after my war. Was this it for me? Would I see it through this battle and move on to another mission? Would I make it through that one? I wondered what I would look like *if* I made it to the other end of my war.

I prayed desperately that I wouldn't end up like my father, physically broken and harmed for life, needing a strong whisky to numb the pain, and then needing another one to prevent the memories, the nightmares of war. I subdued my tears, as I selfishly thought of myself. I already had death and destruction burned into my mind. I was already emotionally deformed.

I took in a deep drag of my cigarette and shuffled the Bren gun resting neatly on my pile of sandbags. The sky was still a midnight blue, as if it had been stained with a dye, just tarnished here and there with darkened clouds. The smell of cordite and death hung forebodingly in the air, while a padre ran around, reading last rites to the wounded, and blessing those of us still alive.

The clouds rolled by swiftly, every now and then passing over the moon and forcing us into a darkness.

The French civilian had begun distributing food and wine, he was celebrating. We had stopped the celebrating for now, the easiest part was over. We waved and shook hands with the man and his family, but that was as far as this liberation party went for us. Every now and then someone would give him a patronising embrace, mixed with a 'Keep your voice down' type of handshake. We had taken the bridge with complete surprise, but now they had had time to reorganise and revaluate, we were all in grave danger.

Still, we didn't turn the bread and the wine down, the ration packs we had been issued might have to last us another week and we didn't know when we might be resupplied. Besides, the wine was good.

Charlie was back by my side. His lower leg was now a darkened brown rather than khaki, and I could tell that the bandage had already begun to fuse to the skin, compensating for the pockmarks of holes that lay beneath. I didn't want to be around when they peeled that off him. He grimaced as the pain of breathing continued to cause him discomfort, and he tugged at the bandage that occupied his arm.

His uniform was ripped and torn, his smock displaying proudly where the snagging wire had ensnared him.

His Sten was rested on top of the sandbags, pointing towards the crossroads, but he was slumped up against our mini fortress, his back facing the same way as his weapon. He looked solemn, locked in his own thoughts, staring at the ground. He twiddled with his fingers for a while, intertwining them with one another before yanking them apart.

I was terrified. They were on their way back, more men would be available to them, heavier weapons. I needed to prepare for death once more.

Despite this, knowing Charlie was sat next to me comforted me. In the short time I had been without him, I had missed him. We'd been together for quite a while. We'd shared a billet when we had been training and got to know each other well. There was no way of being shy with a group of other men if you have to share a toilet with one another for more than twenty-four hours. In fact, it had been more like ten minutes with Charlie and sharing a toilet with him was an experience of war within itself.

He poked his finger down his bandage and began to itch. I hadn't liked him at first, he hadn't liked me. He thought I was too young, despite being a similar age. I thought he was stuck up. He thought I was cocky. I thought he was boring.

He especially couldn't stand the way that I liked to free things up. American chocolate bars, cigarettes, alcohol, you name it and it always managed to find its way to me, and naturally I would offer them up to everyone in the billet, for a price. He had seemed to think that by association, he too would end up in hot water if anyone found out.

Before too long I was found out though, Captain Howarth had approached me to see if I could lay my hands on some American alcohol for a dinner party he was hosting. Through clever negotiation I ended up with three bottles, which placed me firmly in the Captain's good books, even though he only ended up with two bottles, and a promise to turn a blind eye to my mischievous hands.

Not a week later and Charlie was trading goods with me.

I could tell he was thinking about Christine, his body language gave him away. His shoulders would always slump, his head would bow so much his chin would meet with his chest and his arms would rest on the back of his neck. He did it unconsciously, but everyone knew to leave him well alone when he adopted that position.

He was always melancholic when he thought of Christine, at least he was when he was with us, always counting down the days to when he would get to see her again. He was one of the only blokes in the regiment who was actually married. Everyone else, considered themselves far too young for that sort of thing, and set about having as much fun as they possibly could, and getting into as much trouble as they could find.

I felt desperately sorry for him, even though he, in actual fact, felt no worse than me.

I was surrounded by men, my companions, all roughly the same age as me, all in the same boat. But I found it difficult to believe that even half of them were feeling the same way as me, but I knew it to be true.

They all pined for home, they all longed to be reunited with their loved ones. We all had a bond, a union, a sense of togetherness that now we had entered into it, could not be broken merely by bombs and bullets.

But I felt so alone. So awfully alone. A nagging feeling that I did not have what the others had, something that I had imposed upon myself but dreaded that I would regret it. Every time I thought about it, it would send a chill rushing all over my body, a chill that threatened to push the hairs on my arms up, and through my jacket.

I had lied to them, woven a tale of deceitful dishonesty, told them stories that had shaped an image in their minds. I was a good, loyal, wholesome individual, a young man with a woman waiting patiently at home for me.

I had met her at school, our families were friends and we had grown up together. We grew together as we developed through adolescence before we finally realised that the feelings we had for each other were the strong, magnetic pulls of love.

We had become sweethearts, and so I distanced myself from the daily ritual of heading into town to link up with some of the local girls. I would sit quietly, nursing a drink, observing the way the liquid would slosh around and mould to the shape of the glass. Always, with Charlie by my side.

I would contemplate life, reminisce of past times, my childhood, my parents, my friends.

But none of this was down to the fact that I was in love. I had had a girlfriend once it was true, I even based my tales of love on her, but it was all a grand illusion. The fact of the matter was I could barely remember what she looked like.

I had no one. How could I?

The clouds rolled over the light of the moon once more, and as they did so, a chill came over me. I knew I wasn't gaining any warmth from the glare of the moon, but the sudden, haunting darkness that swept over that tiny village, filled my soul with a penetrating cold.

How could I allow someone to learn all about me, my likes and dislikes, my bad habits, my fears and my dreams?

How could I let someone develop feelings for me,

learn to love the unlovable parts of me only for it all to be ripped away when I never came home?

Or worse, how could I let someone fall in love with me, only for me to return a completely different person? My father had changed. Physically *and* mentally. How could I subject someone to what my mother goes through daily, happily reminiscing of days gone by before being struck by a moment of intense despair at the thought of what I had changed into.

I had isolated myself to protect the poor soul who might end up with me.

As I whipped my helmet off and ran my hands through the greasy mess that was my hair, I realised how much of a cynic I had become.

Charlie had often told me about Christine. But I hadn't cared. I wasn't even sure that he was in love. I had begun to convince myself that love didn't actually exist. How could love exist in a world where men can so easily cut each other down with a machine gun? Or nonchalantly toss a grenade into a room where dozens of men may be sleeping? Or launch a loaded Sten gun towards a man with the sole intention of killing him? How could love exist in a world where burning men alive with a flamethrower is just considered another necessity of war? It couldn't.

Len had spoken to me about his life, every aspect of his upbringing, revealed to a near-stranger. But I hadn't listened, I hadn't wanted to. Charlie had been the only person I had connected to, the only one who saw through the window into my mind and understood.

I sighed heavily as I despaired of the person I was becoming. It seemed that nothing could prevent war from changing a person, no matter how hard he tried.

I stopped my train of thought from continuing anymore, I was becoming suicidal. A dangerous place for a man to be in, especially in the middle of a war.

I let the Bren fall to its side gently as I shuffled around in my pocket. Pulling a packet out, I inspected it. The orange wrapping paper glowed in the night sky, its large lettering filling my vision. I'd completely forgotten about it. I was particularly proud of this one, I had stolen it from the back of an American military police jeep in town. It had just been sitting there, staring at me. It would have melted otherwise. Afterwards I thought about how lucky I had been not to be caught, and from then on it had been my charm. It had worked up until this point.

Amongst other things, Company Sergeant-Major Baker had been a big influence on us all, but he had taught me in particular how to keep my head up but, more importantly, how to keep everyone else's head up. He was a good man, a professional soldier, an experienced one and a man that was gracious enough to impart his knowledge to us in a desperate attempt to keep us alive.

"Always carry a treat with you; whiskey, chocolate… anything that you can get your hands on to put a smile on someone's face."

I kicked Charlie gently, trying to avoid his leg. I hoped it would uplift both of us, as we waited for the Germans to return.

Slowly, he turned his head towards me, his eyes filled with tears, bloodshot.

"Here you are, take it," my voice sounded almost alien to me, my throat was dry and I crackled rather than spoke.

He looked at it for a moment, probably deliberating whether it would be worth it considering it had melted and solidified a good four or five times over. I thrust it towards him, beckoning him to take it. A few seconds more of staring, and he grabbed it.

Sporadically, he offered me a few pieces, which I took. The misshapen chocolate tasted wonderful, but it had been so long since I had had some that it seemed foreign to me.

"You're getting your colour back in you mate," I said cheerily, trying to coax him and me out of the cycle of thought. There was no way I could determine the colour of his face, his camo cream had seen to that, but as he scoffed at my poor encouragement, he snapped himself out of the trance he had been in.

He heaved himself to his knees and leant out over the sandbags, towards the cross roads. Leaning his head on top of his hands, he sighed. It felt good to have him back, he had always been at my side, in training, evenings out, meal times, whenever I turned, he would always be within a few yards.

"You know I err…I err…" he struggled to get his thoughts out into words for a moment and seemed to give up.

"I erm…I missed you when I was back there you know. I was praying that you'd be alright." Never once did his gaze defer from staring straight ahead, and I was secretly glad that it didn't.

I let a few seconds pass. It felt good to know that someone else here was worried about me. Maybe I wasn't as alone as I had felt.

"I think now you've lost your chocolate, you're going to need all the prayers you can get," he scoffed. He'd liked that one very much, his jokes always got the biggest laugh from himself.

"How long before you reckon they'll be back," I croaked.

I'd said the wrong thing. He shuffled nervously on the spot before tucking his chin back down into his chest.

We were enveloped in calm once again. It seemed like no one was moving, no one was talking, no one was smoking even. We were all on edge. Hours must have passed and with each minute the uneasiness grew. I could feel the rubber band being stretched and stretched, all of us perched on it, waiting for it to snap, pinging back and whipping us all.

"Maybe they aren't coming back," Charlie wistfully said after what felt like an hour or two. I supressed another yawn and blinked hard to rid myself of the water it built up in my eyes. I wanted desperately to try and get to sleep, but every time I closed my eyes, the gaping wound in the back of Len's head filled my vision, the incessant tapping consuming my ears, stopping only for the roar of the Pole.

Tap. Tap. Tap.

His voice trailed off at the end, as if even he didn't believe what he was saying, trying to make himself sound less stupid. We both knew he was wrong, no matter how much we wanted to believe it, we knew that—

Suddenly, the noise of rising weapons and cocking handles sounded in unison as the faint patter of running footsteps echoed through the plaza. I realigned the Bren with my shoulder, made sure it was cocked, and buried my head on the butt of the weapon, ready to fire. Simultaneously, I felt Charlie do the same, his chest exuding an element of confidence for the first time. I heard him steady himself with his breathing, and as the Bren rose and fell sharply with my chest, I decided to do the same.

I surveyed the darkness, waiting for a figure, or figures, to appear from the abyss, but all I could hear was the faint footsteps. I closed my eyes for a brief moment, trying to reset them, as if that would help as I strained. As I opened them, I made out a figure, vague at first, but before too long the outline became more defined, more focused. I waited for another outline to join the first, followed by another figure and another, as a multitude of men made their way towards us. But the second figure never appeared.

Glancing to my right, I double checked that I had all my spare magazines resting loyally on the top of the sandbags. Our job now was to defend, and to do that, I needed to be spitting out rounds faster than they could spit them back at us. Three magazines sat waiting to do their duty on top of the wall.

Gently, I placed the first pad of my index finger on the trigger, breathing out slowly, I gradually increased the pressure, bringing it close to the point where I would feel it suddenly jolt, as the first round was ejected. I brought the gun sight up so that it was pointing at where I thought the figure's chest should be, and I stared intently as the final fuzzy edges of the figure began to clear. Slowly, I squeezed the trigger some more, bringing it closer to my chest, just a bit more pressure, one final—

"Don't shoot!" came an urgent cry, "It's Johnson!" Almost dropping the Bren to the floor, I made sure my finger was as far away from the trigger as possible. I sucked in vast quantities of air as I calmed myself from almost murdering one of my own.

The terrified figure came surging forward and passed us at a lightning speed. He wore no webbing, no helmet and carried no weapon. The speed he was travelling at showed how light he was compared to the rest of us. His footsteps began to recede as Johnson charged onwards, powered by his sense of purpose.

I suddenly felt very self-conscious about how tight my own webbing was. Surely the perils of the chocolate hadn't taken hold around my waistline already? I pulled at the buckle and loosened it by a notch or two, all the while trying to get some cool air around my body, to rid myself of the sweat.

Johnson had made it to the far end of the bridge by the time I had finished adjusting my webbing.

"What do you reckon is happening?" queried Charlie. He didn't need an answer, he knew what was happening. When a messenger charges over to the most superior officer on the ground in the middle of a war, it doesn't exactly mean it's good news.

There wasn't even time to issue a 'Stand To' order, the light squeal of tank tracks as they trundled their way down the street was already wafting to our ears. Johnson had done well to not be seen by them, and also outrun them.

A few men with heavier weaponry, PIAT guns and anti-tank grenades changed where they were positioned, so they were able to look down the road more clearly.

"Hold fire chaps," came a cry, "lure them onto the bridge if necessary".

The reassuring tones of the major did nothing to stop the trembling in my hand. The heavier guns were all well and good, but they often misfired, weren't powerful enough and were operated by teenagers who had never fired one in anger before. We were to let them onto the bridge, and from there, they would occupy our killing zone. No one would survive the onslaught of the fireworks that would ensue. Except perhaps a twenty-five tonne, twenty-three-foot-long tank with two machine guns and a three-inch self-propelled gun.

Reluctantly, Charlie replaced his helmet, after he'd had a good old scratch at his scalp and sluggishly raised his weapon too. It was as if he was on another training exercise, and he'd just been woken to take his turn on watch.

If the tank made it to where we were, Charlie and I were next to useless with our weapons. We'd have to wait for the big boys to do their bit and wait till our opportunity arose. Tanks worried me. Not because of their great barrels that you saw before the rest of it, not even because of what happened to Dad, but because we had been trained to fight hand to hand with their occupants. Boarding them like deranged pirates and take them on, man versus man.

A corporal ran about, visiting every sandbag pit, slit trench and wherever else men sought cover.

He skidded into us.

"Heads down. Don't let them see you," he'd barely finished his sentence before he was charging across to another Bren on the opposite side of the crossroads to us.

I pulled the Bren off the sandbags and slumped down the other side of the wall. I kept the butt tucked firmly into my shoulder, ready to swing over at the drop of a hat and rain red hot bullets down on the enemy. All feelings of guilt and conscience seemed to subside as anger and aggression took over.

Why were we hiding? They knew exactly where we were. Why would we take the bridge and leave? Why would we let them play hide and seek with us? What was to stop them from driving within range of the bridge and blast everything that offered any kind of cover into oblivion? Why weren't we standing up to fight?

The tank was getting closer. The scurrying footsteps of the corporal got more and more infrequent before they slowed to a complete stop. The only sound now was the tank tracks. Everything else was drowned out by its horrifying squeal.

I wanted desperately to peep over the top and take a look at what was going on, but I knew I couldn't. I was too scared anyway.

Whatever was about to happen, whether it be hordes of men accompanying the steel beast, or one of the PIAT guns heroically taking out the tank, it would all be played out through my hearing.

Sergeant-Major Baker had often imparted advice to me about how to survive, he had told me to identify my dark place, the point at which I felt like I couldn't go on any further and to prepare myself to push through it, that would be what kept me alive. Until this point, I had never experienced as dark a place as this, but now I was there, I could see no way out, I couldn't push through it.

My eyes were now obsolete. I clamped them shut, keeping them closed till the stinging stopped. I pulled my knees tight into my chest and rested my chin on them, like a child sulking. My legs began to bounce up and down, I tried to consciously control the quiver, but as the tank grew closer, I realised it was the ground that shook, and not me. I felt almost relieved with myself.

The tracks got closer, the low monotonous rumbling of the engine, hammering my ears. I took slow, deep breaths and tried to clear my mind.

I made a very conscious effort to prevent myself from emptying my bowels all over the floor.

The engine grew to a crescendo and stopped. He'd reached the crossroads. The idling engine haunted me for what felt like forever.

Any second now a high velocity round would penetrate the sandbags and throw me across the bridge. I would become a ravished corpse, limbs lying several feet from the rest of me as I gasped out my last few, pitiful breaths.

At least I would die alongside Charlie. I glanced at him. I wish I hadn't. He began shuffling to his feet, eyes fixed directly in front of him like a madman.

I felt for my lucky chocolate bar.

PART II

1

6th June 1944
01.37 hours

MY MIND COULDN'T SEEM to focus with the intense burning sensation that filled my eyes while I rested them. Great droplets of water rushed to flood them before bursting their banks and seeping out of the corner of my eyelids. I tried to move my arms up to press my fingers onto my eyelids to rub them clear, but my arms were too heavy to result in any sort of action.

My vision was hazy as I blinked furiously, trying to return it back to normal.

The sky was still an inky, midnight blue colour when I finally found the energy to unclamp my eyelids. It seemed calm, a few wispy clouds hung limply in the sky, pushed gently by the breeze as I followed one cloud before I could see it no longer.

My eyelids felt heavy and cumbersome, almost like the wire cutters had done, and they threatened to close again as I lost control of them completely.

I was given a new energy as a shooting star zipped across the sky, coming from the bottom of my vision and shot out of my view. Lying on my back, I watched with excitement and amusement as another one pinged across the night sky, followed by another and another. I laughed and cheered as I watched the astrological phenomenon unfold before my very eyes.

"George!" I found myself calling, "George! Come and look at this!" My little brother had always been fascinated by the stars, the two of us spending hours flat on our backs staring at the sky as he taught me what each one was called. He was intelligent, my little brother, one of those children who picked up everything immediately. He was destined for some great things. He was always smiling, his smile having to fight against the slightly chubby face that he possessed. His cheeks burned an intense red colour, never changing, with his eyes set against them, the deepest blue you had ever seen. He was, in the eyes of everyone who met him, perfect. And, it was true, he was certainly destined for greatness. If he hadn't been killed.

My yells were cut short as I realised I was moving, dragged backwards as my back began grating against cold steel. I cranked my neck back as far as I could, to see what force was heaving me away from the show put on for me by the stars.

I caught a glimpse up a pair of nostrils, before he turned his head down to me, grimacing and grunting. When he realised I had seen his face, the grimacing turned to grinning and the grunting ceased.

"You're alright mate, keep your eyes up here, keep them here."

"Keep your eyes up here," could only mean one thing; my lower body was a mess. I couldn't feel any pain, no resistance in my lower body to suggest I was injured, the only pain I was experiencing was courtesy of this man, as he tugged me around by my webbing, cutting furiously into my armpits.

My face must have reflected the pure horror that I anticipated, as he started joking with me.

"Oh, I'm not that ugly am I mate? I'm trying to 'elp!"

Somehow, I resisted the childlike urge to take a glance down at my legs and kept my focus solely on my rescuer.

The medics that had accompanied us on our landing were a good bunch of guys, they had all seen combat before and seemed to know exactly what they were talking about. But being dragged around by one of them was never a particularly good sign.

The hairs of his nostrils filled my attention once again as he returned to putting in all his effort in yanking me around. They flicked around wildly as he sighed aggressively with each sudden, painful, pull.

I tried to kick my legs and buck around in protest but only achieved in throwing my shoulders around wildly, like a captured animal. I felt pathetic, once again I had become someone else's responsibility, someone else's burden. First, Company Sergeant-Major Baker, Charlie, then Len, followed by my mysterious, murderous saviour. Now, it was the medic. I could not fend for myself.

"Woah mate, woah, we're nearly in cover," he continued to try and calm me, but only succeeded in infuriating me more, treating me like some kind of wounded horse.

The shooting stars had turned into aggressive tracer rounds, flying in every direction, disappearing behind the medic's head sporadically. Slowly, my mind adjusted to the *snap snap snap* of machine gun fire as it aimed for one man dragging another. Or maybe it was returning fire in our favour. I couldn't tell.

The *snap snap snap* began to distort itself in my mind as it slowly became a *tap tap tap* of a fingernail on a hard surface and the image of a gaping, sucking, bloody wound flashed through my mind quicker than one of the tracers ever could.

The more I focused on the *snap snap snap* the less I focused on the other noises around me. I gave myself a mental slapping and retuned my senses to take in as much information as I could.

The gunfire was instantly drowned out by a contorted mixture of shrieking and hollering as men lay strewn all about the place.

My head began swivelling around like a hyperactive owl, as I started to piece together what was happening.

Men lay howling on the ground all around me, grappling with the floor as they tried to crawl to safety. Some lay motionless, face down on the ground, arm outstretched as they gave in, unable to pull themselves any further.

I was pulled past a torso, chest pointing proudly to the sky, the rest of that human jigsaw puzzle must have been lying close by.

I stared in awe as a silhouette charged forwards, grabbed an inanimate body and began heaving him backwards in the same manner as I was travelling, only to be cut short as a burst of gunfire seemed to explode outwards from his chest, leaving his body a crumpled heap on the floor.

I recognised one of the corpses as I was dragged past, he was another of the pilots. In life, he had been a bubbly character, the sort of bloke who would always be up for a laugh and never sat down for more than a minute. He'd been the one who'd played the piano the night before we flew, drawing huge roars of laughter as he sang 'I haven't seen old Hitler,' each verse getting faster than the last, to the point where he was red in the face. In death, his face was already going a vague bluish colour, the life sapped out of his eyes already, the glint that used to be so prominent, dried up.

Tap. Tap. Tap.

"There we are mate, wait there, I'm going back for your buddy."

He was a Cockney, just like me, I was sure of it, but I didn't have time to ask him before he left me lying desperately in a slit trench as his footsteps receded away into the firestorm.

A shockwave pulsated down the right side of my body as if I had just gripped onto a live electrical wire. I instantly felt the explosion of pain in my skull as my body reacted in the quickest way possible by implementing more pain in my rapidly weakening body. Throwing my head back in agony, I smashed my skull into the concrete reinforcements around me. My helmet had gone.

My arm throbbed, and my leg was pure agony. Chancing a look at my arm I instantly regretted my decision. My arm seemed intact from the fingers upwards, but where there should have been a crease in my arm, a great chunk was missing, as if I had been bitten by a savage wolf. I now knew why I had found it so difficult to move my arm, I could see inside it. I blinked furiously for a moment or two before glancing away and taking a look at my leg.

The pain wasn't so great at first, but the longer I stared at it, the more aggressive the stabbing became. I could see sinews and individual strands of muscle that before was protected by a layer of skin. Large shards of glass and brick seemed to be sticking out of my shin, more precisely, my shinbone.

The bone stared at me for a while, willing me to look away first, which I did. I let out a great roar of agony, a great crescendo that any lion would have been proud of, the pathetic weeping maybe not so much. I sucked in air sharply and exhaled it just as quickly again, trying to keep my mind off the nausea that was slowly coming over me.

My childlike weeping was soon drowned out by another, more determined cry of anguish. Like a child fighting for attention, I knew I was beaten, and my weeping turned to a resigned sob. I couldn't help but feel compassion for the poor soul on the end of that cry, his wounds a more immediate concern than mine.

I watched intently as the back of the medic appeared over the top of the trench.

Never ending pleas of "help me, help me," were met with sympathetic, almost maternal-like tones.

"Alright mate, we're here."

As the medic began fiddling in his bag, and tending to the wounds of his new patient, I leant on my left side and pulled myself over to see what I could do to help.

We had wanted to coax the tank on to the bridge and

take it out. Something must have gone wrong with our plan.

The blast must have come from somewhere, it didn't matter exactly where from, just that it had most definitely come.

2

6th June 1944

I WAS QUITE TAKEN ABACK when the medic near enough manhandled me back to the ground when he realised I was trying to get up and about. His sympathetic tones completely disappeared, and he bullied me back to where he wanted me.

"I'll look at you in a minute! Stay still!"

He screamed so loudly that great balls of phlegm shot out of his mouth and landed neatly on my cheek. The sounds of the machine guns, ticking away like clocks gone mad, were felt rather than heard, as they reverberated and throbbed through my entire being. I sensed every projectile as it ripped through the night air, before slamming itself suicidally into something, living or not, they didn't care.

I could begin to make out commands and the odd encouragement as presumably the boys had recovered from the initial shock of the blast. The crescendo grew louder and louder as a more concerted effort to repel the enemy took hold.

It was at times like this that the injured hero would give a shout of "Go on boys! Let 'em have it!" But I didn't much feel like a hero right now, nor was my morale high enough to be so optimistic.

"Please do more, do something else, please…anything."

One quick blast had done it for me and this poor fellow, and probably more besides were still sprawled out there as a result. Maybe there had been more than one blast, I had no idea how many of our boys were still out there giving it their all.

"Get me home, please."

For all I could make out, they might have been behind us, and we were the frontline. I tensed up at the thought of a German soldier peering down into this slit trench at the three of us, not one of us armed. The tension in my body caused an upsurge in pain and I couldn't help a grunt passing my lips.

That got the medic's attention as he soon turned to me and began cleaning and bandaging my wounds.

"That's the best I can do for now bud, sorry."

"Don't matter." I chanced a grin, "I've had worse."

His mouth curled up one side and he exhaled through his nose sharply, he'd heard that one before.

He turned back to his other patient, just as an overwhelming sense of guilt washed over me.

"Charlie!" I screamed at the top of my voice, "Charlie!" I felt a blood vessel or two burst in the back of my throat as I hollered, a combination of the unusual strain on my voice and the desperate thirst that I found myself enduring.

I'd forgotten about him, and not for the first time. I'd left him out there on his own, I'd let him down again. I mustered all my energy and ignored the pain as I tried to shift myself, at least into an upright position. All I could think about was myself, I had been engulfed in a selfishness that I had never before experienced. I had lacked any concern for the other wounded, the medic risking his life for me and most of all Charlie. It was becoming a frequent habit.

"I'm a bit busy Johnny mate," his reply was strained and interrupted by agonising sighs.

The medic turned again as he sensed me sit up, but this time he didn't bundle me to the ground. He had turned just enough so that I could see his patient. I felt grateful to the medic, he had dragged me quite some distance, under fire, before plonking me in this trench to tend to me. I wanted to grab his hand and shake it vigorously as a display of my appreciation, but my gaze was fixed firmly on the body that lay in front of him.

His left eye had seemed to have completely moulded into the rest of his face, it simply wasn't there anymore. The rest of his face looked as though it had been dried out thoroughly and peeled backwards, as if only the thinnest sheet of skin protected his face. I could see quite clearly the bones that constructed his face, and his nostrils seemed enlarged, like the nose itself had been reduced in size.

The skin on his neck had creased up and was bright red, except for one vein that protruded defiantly against the rest of his skin.

"Maybe...maybe they'll let me join the Guinea Pig

Club now, eh?" he tried to laugh but instead winced as the medic checked his pulse once more. His voice faltered and I instantly knew he was crying, although, in the darkness of the night, I could see no tears streaming down his face.

It was a long-standing joke that we'd had, that if my dad had been in the RAF he would have gained access to the Guinea Pig Club, a drinking club for burns victims. It was a joke that masked my true fear over the possibility of the same happening to me.

The pain my dad had been in must have been excruciating. Yes, I lived with it every day of my childhood growing up, watching my father clamp down on his lip as he tried to prevent another howl from emanating from his mouth, but I'd never had to experience the pain. Growing up with my dad in the way that he was had made me fear something. I was not scared of death, I would know nothing of it if I never woke in the morning, but it was the pain that scared me, the agonising process of dying that chilled me.

Except it wasn't happening to me.

He screamed in agony again as the medic tried to tend to his injuries. Soon after, he began to shake, violently. I shuffled around the medic, trying to gain a more permanent view of my friend, and it was then that it hit me. It smelled like burning rubber to me at first, but as I let the smell develop in my nostrils, I soon realised that it was a putrid, sickening smell, a scent that I would never want to smell again, for as long as I lived. Burnt flesh.

Tap. Tap. Tap. The sucking gut wound. The crater in the skull. The burning flesh.

"He needs fluids, fast. We need to move him but that might make matters worse."

He was flustered, I couldn't blame him, anyone would be when faced with a moral dilemma in such close proximity to a patient. It was unnerving, he had been here before, tending to a wounded man under intense fire, but this one was different for him. It was affecting him. Watching him flap around like a nervous puppy filled me with nothing but discomfort and dread.

"His pulse is up," he was talking to me as if I was a colleague, a senior doctor.

"What do we do?" I refrained from adding the addendum "if anything," that had popped into my mind. We *would* get Charlie out. We simply *had* to.

He pursed his lips for a moment or two before looking up, directly into my eyes. I hated it when people did that. Slowly, deliberately, he shook his head from side to side and shrugged.

"There's too many possible consequences…" he trailed off, before pointing out of the slit trench just as another grenade, as if on cue, dumped all of its explosives with a *thump*.

I couldn't tell if he knew what was going on but, Charlie began to weep again, before his weeps slowly turned to anguished sobs.

"Please Johnny…Will you get me some help? Will *you* help me?"

"The adrenaline is wearing off, he's going to be even worse in a minute," he spoke as if Charlie was in a separate room to us, completely unaware of our presence.

He began to writhe around, as if he was possessed, his face twisting and contorting in ways that didn't seem human. His screams became more agonising to listen to as they began to etch themselves into my brain, they were never ending, consumed by the possibility of an unceasing pain.

Tap. Tap. Tap.

His chest heaved up and down as he struggled for air, before his stomach constricted as he vomited over the medic's feet.

He was barely recognisable, he had no facial features anymore, just a barren wasteland of skin, a searing red colour, that seemed to move like a bowl of water as he screamed and recoiled in pain.

I felt selfish as I thought of Dad. I wondered how he had reacted when he had first been burnt. I had a romantic picture in my mind of his bravery and how he remained largely unaffected by what had happened to him, but I knew it can't have been true.

"We've got to try something!" I screamed, now sobbing, and not as a result of my own injuries.

As Charlie lay there, I couldn't help but feel that my Dad had in fact, been one of the fortunate ones. He came home. As the seconds wore on, it was more and more evident that Charlie wasn't going to be one of them.

All of a sudden, the gunfire stopped. I couldn't tell if it had stopped suddenly or if I had only just noticed it. Either way, the medic had noticed it at the same time too and jerked his head up like a meerkat.

"Wait here, I'm going for a stretcher."

He hopped up and over the lip of the trench and got no more than a few yards before his head reappeared.

"I'll make that two," I shuffled around in a futile attempt to argue back with him, but he had already vanished.

Charlie's screams, like the gunfire, now ceased in a flash. I turned to look at him.

His eyes were bloodshot, and he blinked slowly, as if he was dropping off to sleep. I gripped hold of his arm, one of the only places that looked like it would remain intact if I touched it.

"Mate," I pleaded with him. I didn't want him to die, I at least wanted the medic here with me if he did.

He looked calm, like he was suddenly at peace with the world. With tears in his eyes he began to whisper, softly at first, but then louder as if it was for my benefit.

The same word, over and over again, taking up all of his might to utter each syllable, each syllable vitally important to him.

The same name, over and over.

"…Christine…Christine…Christine…".

3

June 1944

I HAD SPENT the journey back to England counting the number of bolts that I could see in the wall opposite my bed on the hospital ship. I needed something, anything to take my mind off what had happened. I counted. I checked and re-checked. Then I'd start all over again. The whole way back.

We wouldn't be getting the hero's welcome most of the men on this ship deserved. *I* certainly didn't deserve it. I had failed.

My job was to fight alongside those men to the very best of my ability, to stop the German counter-attack and hold the bridge. I had been taken out in the very first moment of the attack. I had failed.

I could have done more to prevent my best friend, my only friend from getting injured, from suffering the horrific burns that he had to endure. His paper-thin skin was all that occupied my mind, great blisters taking up what was left of it.

My leg was on the mend, it sat in a splint from my ankle to my hip, a great long train track stretched right up the front of my shin where the stitches had left their mark. My arm sat in a sling. That would take a tad longer to heal. Every time I moved, the weeping wound would drip again, a light pus to begin with, before graduating to the thicker, scarlet liquid that I was now so accustomed to seeing dripping from a man.

A wheelchair was my mode of transport for the time being, entirely dependent on someone else's mercy as they wheeled me from one room to the next. Helping me into bed or my pyjamas, feeding me my food or helping me pee. I felt humiliated from the time I woke up, to the time that I would try to sleep. The time that I succumbed to the nightmares.

Being transported about in the wheelchair, would become a new low for me. The feeling of utter worthlessness that I experienced was one that I found incredibly difficult to combat. I had relied on people so much to this point and here again, I found myself utterly dependant on another human being.

I had been knocked about a fair bit while being carted around in the chair, the occasional "sorry mate," from the orderly was no compensation for the pain that would ensue. The arms of the chair would be worn away by the time I left it, the skin on my bottom lip in a similar condition, a consequence of the biting down and the clamping of nails when yet another person would knock my arm or trip on my leg.

I wasn't sure if I even needed the help, but my mind was so exhausted I wasn't sure if I could command my limbs to do anything. I couldn't sleep.

Charlie was dead. A shiver encompassed my body every time I thought of the reality of what had happened. I had escaped lightly, I would walk again, I would write again. I would go home.

In my dreams, Charlie lay next to me, at the bottom of that slit trench, in Northern France. There was no gunfire, no screams, no horrific injuries. Just us two. We had trained together, lived together, laughed together. We had flown into France together. Now we lay there, in the trench…together.

Death would stand over us, just watching us at first, our breathing mainly, the way our chests fell and rose like the most ferocious storm in an ocean. His lips, his thin lips, would begin to curl, like a small piece of thread, snarling upwards in a sneer. He was deliberating which soul he would take with him that night.

People tried to talk to me about how I had ended up where I was, they seemed proud, excited almost that they had come so close to death and yet survived. Some were even eager to get on the first ship back to France. But no words came out of my mouth. Nothing.

"He's just exhausted," said one nurse when the body occupying the bed next to me kicked up a fuss. I was, she was right, I hadn't slept a wink in the three weeks or so that I had been laid up in France while they decided what to do with me.

My mind raced for my every waking moment. What had happened. What could have happened. What might still happen. I thought of it all.

There were thirty-seven bolts from what I could see of this particular segment of the ship. Thirty-seven. An odd number. I tapped my fingers on the arms of the wheelchair in frustration, *why only thirty-seven?* It took me all my might to tear myself away from staring at the wall, growing increasingly angry at whoever hadn't put one final bolt in to make an even number.

Soon after docking, I was wheeled in front of a Major Lewis, a man who seemed to sit hunched over his desk so much that he was permanently locked in a position staring down at his notepad. His white coat over the top of his khaki uniform reassured me somewhat, maybe he could confirm what was going on inside my head.

The room that Major Lewis occupied was like a school sports hall, the bland, unremarkable walls feeling like they were closing in on me from all sides. Other medical staff seemed undistractedly busy as they sprinted about, rushing to the aid of a fallen man, or to mop up a pool of blood that had found its way to the floor.

Tables with army personnel occupying them, lined one of the long walls, each with a worn away piece of flooring where the wheelchairs or walking sticks had slowly battered them.

The room was busy, maybe fifty people hustling and bustling their way around the hall. As I approached my table however, everyone else seemed to vanish.

"Any other symptoms other than the arm and the leg?" He barely looked up from his notepad, scribbling furiously. The constant scratching of the nib on the paper began to wear me down, as I watched it bob up and down in his hand. He continued to scratch away, nothing comprehensible from what I could see, just vague shapes in a fading ink, on a yellowing piece of paper. The frustration at his lack of communication with me was reaching boiling point. My fingers began incessantly tapping on the arm, and my good leg began jerking up and down as if I had a tremor.

With each scratch of his nib, with each tap on the floor as the orderlies walked around, it felt as if a wasp was stinging me. The wasp would hover for a moment, before striking, retreating slightly, before slamming itself into me once again. But this wasp wasn't going for my skin, it was going for my mind, my sanity.

My frustration with Major Lewis' scratching nib and the other, inconsiderate, incessant noises around me, slowly began to turn to anger, pure aggression began surging around my body with every heartbeat, like some sort of toxin.

"Why does he have to be making that noise?" I began asking myself, *"Why is he being so selfish? Why won't he stop?"*

I knew I was losing my mind, I knew I was being completely irrational, but all I wanted to do was escape, all I wanted to do was run.

But I couldn't, and that was making the rage bubble and boil even more.

My chest began to get tighter and tighter as the scratching continued, and I began to clamp down hard on my back teeth as the tapping seemed to intensify. The murderous aggression and the thoughts that went with it began to cloud my mind completely. All I could do was think about how to end it.

Tap. Tap. Tap. Scratch. Scratch. Scratch. Gut wound. Skull. Burning flesh.

My good fist smashed into the table so hard it nearly went through the desk and out the other side.

"WILL YOU STOP SCRATCHING," I shook violently as I tried to calm myself, placing my bad hand over the good to prevent the shaking. Everyone in the room had come to a complete stop.

My breathing shook in unison with my body as I spluttered an apology to everyone who could hear my crackling speech.

The Major took his spectacles off and waited for me to calm myself down. The tears began splashing onto the Major's desk as I tried in earnest to force them back into my eyes.

"Just breathe son, breathe," his tone more one of impatience than reassurance.

He waited a moment, looking me up and down all the while, waiting for his time.

"So," he uttered a little more calmly this time, and without the scratching nib, "any other issues apart from the arm and the…" he didn't finish his sentence but instead used his pen to point in the direction of my splinted limb. He raised a doctor-like, sympathetic eyebrow, the kind that tells you off for being so foolish in the first place.

Keeping one hand firmly on top of the other, I leant out of my wheelchair slightly, so that I could bend in to him and tell him quietly.

I tried to blink and shut away the tears, but they refused to reopen as I spoke.

"I have…I have…erm…trouble, t-t-trouble sleeping Sir, and erm…" I hesitated, my whole body tensing up and my breathing threatening to give in. A lump of mucus convened at the back of my throat, making my voice stick.

As I struggled to swallow it down, I cleared my throat perhaps a bit too violently for Major Lewis. He sat back from me.

My speech staggered before picking up an unbelievable pace, making me wonder whether he would even be able to take in what I was saying to him.

"I have these dreams, Sir. People dying, people alive who I know to be dead." My eyes darted every which way as I spoke, only bringing them up to his when I'd finished my sentence.

He looked me in the eye and I thought for a moment I sensed a brief notion of compassion from him in his eyes, before he dropped his head back down to his notepad and scratched away once more.

"It's battle fatigue son. Plenty of you boys have it, you'll be right as rain in a couple of months."

I felt like pulling my hair out and simultaneously forming a circle with my hands, my thumbs pressing down sharply on his windpipe until he agreed that what I had was different, different to what plenty of other boys have. I wanted to drain out his arrogance, I wanted to watch his eyes bulge as he realised that he would die. I felt like staying clamped down on his airways until his lips turned a blue-purple colour as the life was slowly sapped out from him.

No, more than that, I wanted him to follow me, to follow me in my dreams as I climbed up that staircase and crouched next to a dying Pole. I wanted him to be with me as I stared in disbelief at a crater in the back of someone's skull. I wanted him to watch a burning man die. I wanted him to be that Pole, to be that cratered skull, to be that burning man.

But most of all, I wanted to stop the unrelenting, enraging, scratching.

I felt nauseous as I fought with my breathing once again to remain conscious. I swayed in my chair as I battled to regain control.

Scratch. Scratch. Scratch.

What I had was deep. Deeper than fatigue, I could feel it in my soul. Fatigue doesn't last, but I could tell this would, till the very day I die. The sounds, the smells, the bodies. My anger towards him subsided as a shaking hand made its way through my greasy, matted hair, I had given up.

Tap. Tap. Tap.

Great barrels of tears cascaded down my cheeks as the Major ushered a nurse in to wheel me away to my next hospital bed. As I reversed, he whipped off his specs once more and looked at me.

"Every man who goes to war dies, son. Anyone who makes it back, comes back cheated."

He meant that. I wondered if he had felt cheated and asked myself what he may have been through. He looked old enough to have fought in the last war, maybe he had. Or maybe he had seen so many of the wounded, broken men from this one, that he had slowly lost his belief in humanity. As I was wheeled helplessly out of the hall, I felt a twang of sorrow for Major Lewis.

The scratching nib picked up pace again.

4

July 1944

THE FIELD HAD a covering of dew over it, which just glistened in the light of the moon. Turning my head, I caught a glimpse of a sodden cobweb, stretching from one tree trunk to another, sparkling sweetly in the night. It seemed almost to glow in the moonlight and was only visible because of the moisture that clung to it. It would be practically invisible by midday.

I pushed my finger into it softly and let it encompass my finger as the spider woke, scurried across its web to investigate, before retreating back into the crevice of the nearby tree.

It was cold, the kind of cold that you can't shake off, no matter how many layers you pull on. The coolness of the night was biting, biting at my skin causing my hairs to stand to attention. But it went deeper than that, the cold tonight was biting my insides, making my blood run as cold as an autumnal river.

A few of the others stirred and grumbled in their sleep as they fought with Mother Nature to get some shut eye. I couldn't sleep, I never could, not even in my own dreams. After a couple of hours, the Captain passed round to inspect us all, making sure we were still alert.

His hunched-up figure was comical against the back-drop of the moon, his silhouette making him appear more like a Greek mythical creature, rather than an officer in His Majesty's Armed Forces.

"Evening chaps, how we all doing?"

A few murmurs of jovial discontent sparked up, which the Captain knew to take with a light heart.

"Well, with any luck boys, Jerry will be getting up soon, they'll keep you awake."

He trudged off again into the dark as the rest of us resettled in for the night.

Before long, the darkness of the night began to surrender to the orangey hues of the morning, tainted by the great pillars of grey that encompassed the sky. I begged the clouds to apart, but even for a moment, just to allow the sun to gently kiss my skin and warm me to the core.

I watched as Company Sergeant-Major Baker appeared, clutching a bottle of whiskey, which was grate-fully passed round to all those still awake.

Can't be long left on my stag now. Sun's rising.

I fought against my senses to shut my eyes for longer than they should. My mind became foggier than the early morning mist and I consciously felt the weight of each individual eyelash. They began drooping, and a sudden shockwave went through my body, forcing my eyes open as I panicked that that last blink had lasted a millisecond or two longer than it should have done.

"Oi, you see that?"

"What?"

"Movement, up there, on the ridge line," his speech was robotic, totally emotionless.

I pulled a pair of clumpy, battered binoculars up to my eyes, but they seemed so knackered that nothing ever appeared closer with them. I tossed them to one side and followed his finger with my naked eye.

The morning mist was just consolidating itself, kissing the top of the slow, steady incline to the top of the hill. The vibrant colours of the morning had been smothered by the icy blanket of the mist, everything turning into a stony grey haze.

"Yeah, I see him."

A lone figure had appeared in the clearing of the woods, small at first, but soon he was charging towards us.

"Do we take him; do we take him?" came the excited chipper beside me. He'd never been under fire before, the whole stag he'd had his finger hovering over the trigger, tapping it gently in a cocktail of nerves and excitement. The barrel of his weapon had been hopping around all night, the end of his gun pointing wherever his manic eyes commanded it next.

I hesitated, waiting to see what happened first.

Bang!

"I got him, I hit 'im!"

I flicked my head furiously to one side, but simultaneously the world exploded around me, flashes of muzzles and tracer fire everywhere. It was spectacular.

I pulled the trigger sharply and a round kicked out of

my rifle, sending it flying backwards into my shoulder and sending a quiver down my spine. I loved that feeling, such a feeling of power and excitement. I could stop anything, anyone.

Machine guns opened up all around me, spitting furious hornets towards the enemy that was engulfing the clearing ahead of us.

Tap. Tap. Tap.

Great numbers of rounds were poured on them, but they kept coming. Hordes upon hordes of men surged towards us, a never-ending supply of cannon fodder. It was futile. There seemed to be thousands upon thousands of them. We would never be able to hold them all back. But there were plenty of us, pouring explosives and rifle rounds on them. They would lose so many men.

I expected to see them, as they normally did, catapulted backwards in a demented cartwheel before lying motionless on the ground, but none of them seemed to drop. I aimed at another unsuspecting victim and pulled the trigger. I watched intently as he too, failed to fall to the ground and I hastily re-cocked my rifle and took aim for a second time.

My aim was off, the mist clouding my vision and my effectiveness.

Again, he continued to charge towards me and I went through the motions once more. My rifle jammed, the bolt wouldn't slide back into place like it was meant to. I pulled it all the way out and back in again, but for a second time it stubbornly refused to move. My fingers began shaking uncontrollably, as if they were possessed. I let my rifle fall limply to the ground and I watched as my hands convulsed fiercely in front of me.

Every fibre of my being was telling me to run, screaming at me to get away, but my legs refused, they simply did not work, the stitches were still there, preventing all movement.

My neighbour fired round after round into him, firing and re-cocking his rifle like a madman, only focused on one thing. But the figure kept coming.

Tap. Tap. Tap.

I scrabbled around, bundling the rifle back into my arms.

I adjusted my vision, keeping my eyes firmly fixed on my opponent, just me and him, as he continued to bound towards me. The guns stopped, it was just me and him. I was all alone, I could make out his face. He was smiling, laughing. A great haunting cackle resounded out across the barren field that would continue in my mind for an eternity.

And then, a voice, softly at first as it seemed to be dulled by the mist.

"…please…please help me…Johnny? You there?"

I felt the mist lift completely as my eyes bulged at the realisation.

It was Charlie.

The lights flicked on. Dad shuffled in, wearing his dressing gown. I was crouched under the kitchen table, and as I dropped my weapon to the floor, it rolled away from me as a rolling pin. My breathing was erratic, and I gave in to the tidal waves of emotion that drowned me.

I sobbed uncontrollably while Dad set about making me a cup of coffee. I watched him through my tears, his silhouette on the wall dancing unpredictably, as he began his day. He sighed as he basked in the warm rays of the early morning, letting them hit him full on in the face through the kitchen window. He spoke, not to me, not even to himself it seemed, he just spoke.

"The world will always be drowning in sorrow and grief. But the sunrise will always be beautiful."

I was back home. Mum went into overdrive as she busied herself making sure that my every need was tended to immediately. Truthfully, it was utter torture.

Dad sat, as he always did, in his chair, smoking and reading the paper from cover to cover and back again. That's exactly what I needed. Normality. I couldn't stand the overbearing nature of my mother, I knew she meant well and only wanted me to recover, but she would have been better off knowing that *nothing* that she did would help me.

I could only sit and smoke, only able to let the warm blanket of the tobacco encompass my lungs, hour after hour, day after day.

The battle was in my mind, not in my physical wellbeing. I struggled to keep my emotions in check during those first few days at home, Mum pushing my patience a lot further than Major Lewis had ever done when I first got off the ship. But she was my Mum, and, despite everything, she was only doing her job, and that thought, it seemed, helped me to calm down somewhat.

What I needed though, was to find someone who felt the same, someone who had experienced what I had and someone that I could talk to. Dad would have been the obvious candidate, but it was clear that we weren't meant to talk about these things for fear of making it worse, and so I pushed it to the back of the queue.

There was a doubt in my mind whether he would have

understood anyway, we'd been in two, very different wars. Dad had been the technological spearhead, but I had been at the tip of a very different spearhead altogether.

I had my parents around me and that's all I wanted when I was in hospital but, now I was with them, I felt alone. Terribly alone.

On the outside I was tired, exhausted; Major Lewis had got that right. But on the inside, I was consumed by a darkness. A darkness I could see no way out of. All I had was myself. And if I could not communicate with myself, how could I expect to communicate with those around me? How could I expect to be my old self, return to normal? Until I learned how to do that, I would be completely on my own.

I had been fighting a righteous war, some of those boys still were. When we came home we were treated as heroes, taking the fight to the enemy and tearing down Hitler's Nazi Germany, foot by foot and yard by yard. Union flags were flown as the men in stretchers and wheelchairs were ushered into the hospital, great whoops and cheers resounded around the room as pictures were shown of our heroes after battle.

People were *proud* of this war. We were fighting a *righteous* war, a *just* one, so why did any man have any right to complain about what had happened? How could I tell people that I had seen an enemy soldier die, but I carried guilt around with me for his death? How could I admit that I no longer felt like I wanted to kill the enemy?

I couldn't. We were fighting a *righteous* war.

5

July 1944

I COULDN'T SLEEP. Every time I did, the same dream would haunt me. The enemy would charge at me, the steely grey uniforms slowly advancing through the early morning mist until everything fell silent. And it was just me and him. Just me and Charlie. Or me and Len. Or the Pole.

They were haunting my dreams, they were haunting my every waking hour.

I couldn't eat. My Mum was a fantastic cook when I was younger, and she continued to be, whipping up great feasts with rationed foods, enough to feed a royal, but I couldn't eat any of it. Every mouthful felt like another spoonful of judgement, or another burden on my back.

It had become a poison to me, settling inside my stomach and slowly rotting away at my very character. It destroyed me, hour by hour, day by day, till I was just a shell of a man, a carcass, no emotions or feelings on the inside other than the despairing guilt of being alive. It was like having a reservoir of petrol inside me, the slightest flicker of a spark setting off a raging fire and destroying me completely.

"You need to get your strength back up, you're skin and bone!"

This was my mother's favourite saying, it always had been, but now she was right. I was losing weight quicker than a stone sinking to the bottom of the ocean.

But I couldn't eat. Every mouthful was another helping of guilt. Why *had* I survived? What had I done to be deemed by the Almighty as worthy of being saved?

I was no different to many of those boys, in fact I had less to live for than them. They had families, wives, children to go back to, to provide for. Instead their families would live on a widow's payoff from the government, while I was free to walk about on the streets.

The disgrace I felt at being alive was overwhelming. I was a coward.

"Dad, I need help," I pleaded as I wasted another afternoon in the armchair staring at the mantelpiece. It was a horrid thing, the mantelpiece, it contained photographs of me from early childhood right up to when I qualified on gliders. At least it did until I smashed it under my boot one evening; Mum had hidden it from me somewhere after that.

He barely looked up from his second reading of the day's newspaper as I begged with him earnestly.

"Dad, how do I cope?"

He waited a moment or two, presumably finishing the

article about Churchill that he had tried to talk to me about earlier. He loved Mr Churchill, something about saving the nation, but I couldn't stand the man. He had sent me to war. He had done this to me.

He cleared his throat as he folded the paper over the arm of his chair.

"Grab your coat son, we're going out."

I followed him down the street, a couple of paces behind him as he stretched his legs further with every stride. His pace picked up the closer we got, like I used to the closer we got to the sweet shop. But the stiffness in my leg kept me at a sobering, slow limp.

He almost brought the pub to a standstill as he clattered in, but before long the patrons had forgotten the madman who bashed his way in, a younger man staggering slowly behind him. They must have written us off as a couple of drunks.

He ordered two half-pints of bitter and walked us both over to a resting point.

He nudged mine over to my side willingly, with a gentle smile and a wink.

"Get it down you mate, it'll make you feel better, I promise."

He wasn't wrong. Before he'd taken another sip, my glass was empty, and he flicked the two glasses round like a trickster, so that my glass was the full one. He gave a sympathetic smile, the sort you give someone as they sob at the loss of a loved one, and you haven't got a clue what to say.

Smiles are fascinating, interesting things, and, although I didn't feel like smiling myself, I needed that smile from my Dad. The human face is an incredibly powerful tool, the slightest change in it can anger and annoy or encourage and reconcile. And that one, from my Dad, in that very brief moment, had pulled me back from the cliff edge, a momentary respite I so desperately needed.

I supped more slowly on my second one, watching as the dark, amber liquid resettled again after each taste. Dad watched with me. As I reached the end of my glass, he began to croak.

"I…I don't…" he said as I looked up at him with an inquisitive eye, "get over it, I mean. I never will."

His eyes were bleary as tears began to well up in them.

"You won't either." I expected those words to be accompanied by a stomach churning wrench, like a boxer had just thumped me in the pit of my stomach, but none of that came. If anything, I was feeling relieved, the tension dissipated.

I had wanted to get over this, I had wanted to forget what I had seen but I knew it was ingrained deep within me. I would *never* forget it.

But somehow knowing that someone else would never get over it, made me feel better, like I wasn't alone, a sort of selfish boasting.

His speech was slow, well thought out, like he was forcing me to digest each syllable, before continuing onto the next.

"They're not all evil Johnny…Not all of them are ruthless killers." His speech was more confident, like he knew this for a fact and I desperately wanted to know why he felt like that. But this conversation was about me, not him, however selfish that may sound.

I longed to know what had happened to him, to know

why he would say such a thing about men who had scarred his body and traumatised his mind.

"The dreams, I still have them. The scars, I still have them too, physical *and* mental. I know I'll never be rid of them."

He let the words sink in for a moment or two before he let out a grunt, accompanied by a straining expression on his face, as he returned to the bar for another round of drinks.

"I used to come in here a lot at first. It helps take the edge off, you know? Helps to reorder the thoughts in your brain."

I nodded as if I knew exactly what he was on about, but my experiences with alcohol had the complete opposite effect on my thought processes. Charlie had been the same. We'd once set fire to a hay bale sat in the middle of a field because Charlie had thought it was a good idea after a few drinks.

I couldn't see how drinking would make anything clear in anyone's head, never mind the things that were zipping through mine.

He was permanently hunched forwards in his chair, no over exaggerated sighs as he leant back like any other Dad imparting advice. This was different from normal fatherly advice, this was advice that no one else in this pub deserved to hear. I couldn't work out if it was this that was making him slope forwards, or the excruciating agony he might feel if he was to lean backwards.

"You won't ever get over it mate. Your mum thinks I am, that I have the occasional dream, the occasional flash-back, but she doesn't know the half of it. Every single day I question myself over why I wasn't killed. I ask whether

I've done enough in my life since to justify the fact that I lived."

He looked at me for a response.

"I don't think I have." I couldn't do anything but sit and stare at my glass. I'd spent hours doing it before, observing the smoothness of the glass, the way that the liquid inside sloshed around like a tornado as I swirled it. But this time it was different, I felt further away from myself every minute.

"We can't tell people, son," he repressed a sob and passed it off as a belch as he got a few looks, "'scuse me," he chuckled, raising an apologetic hand.

"They don't know what it's like," he said nodding towards the other attendees at the bar, "they never will, but they expect us to be proud, proud of ourselves and proud of our mates. But it's…it's difficult."

"They'll never know what it's like and you'll…you'll struggle to cope with that, but you'll have times that you are so intensely happy that it was you that did it, and not them."

He let a few minutes pass before he spoke up again. I could tell he enjoyed talking to me in this way, he had felt like this for more than twenty years. I was the first person he was able to talk to that had a vague understanding of what he had seen and done, and even then, I didn't have a clue. It was all just a story to me, like mine would be a story to him.

He sighed as he tried to flick himself from an unstable, emotional soldier, to a fully functioning, normal husband again. Before he fully made the transition however, he piped up one final time.

"We've all just got to tackle our demons head on. Face

up to them, you know? We shouldn't hide them to ourselves. We shouldn't pretend that they're not there." He spoke with such a conviction, such authority, that I struggled to comprehend how a man so tough had suffered within himself, for this long.

He was off and up, tapping the table as he did, encouraging me to drink up and follow him. I did as I was told and scurried across the pub to catch up with him.

"See ya Frank," called the landlord as we reached the door, and with a flick of the hand in response, we headed for home.

We've just got to tackle our demons, head on.

I lay awake on my bed that night, a welcome change from sitting bolt upright in the armchair. It was the first time I had brought myself to lie on my back since *that* night.

I couldn't sleep as usual, but I felt a tranquillity come over me, a relaxed air surrounded me. I felt reassured, my mind was still all over the place and I knew that, like the world, peace cannot ensue unless there are no wars, but at least, there was a cessation of war, at least in my mind, and the façade of peace came to the fore, just for one night.

I needed to face up to my problems, to come to terms with what had happened and to try and return to society, like a normal person. Besides, I hadn't been discharged yet and I certainly wasn't going to be allowed to take leave indefinitely, one day I would have to return to the war.

I was haunted by Charlie. I had got away, and he hadn't. I needed to face up to him, I needed to be able to tell myself that *he* knew there was nothing I could do for him. He needed to know that I had not chosen to be the one to survive.

But Charlie was dead. How could I face up to a dead man? How could I possibly talk to him?

I lay for a few hours more, thinking about *that* night, but for once I stayed where I was. I had a memory of it, but I wasn't actually *reliving* it.

Suddenly, a thought came to me, and I knew exactly how to face up to it.

And, with that, for the first time in a long time, I fell asleep.

6

August 1944

THE DEEP THROBBING SENSATION, that sent pulsations up your body through the ground returned to me as I entered the village. It was a noise that I hadn't heard for a long time now, but one that I instantly recognised and one that I was strangely at peace with.

It felt good to be back down in Dorset. There was an atmosphere of cleanliness here, the freshness of the air was fresher than the air at home. It made me feel free and replenished. I felt good, these last few nights as I prepared to travel down I had slept and slept well at that. I hadn't had any dreams in anticipation of what was to come. I felt peaceful, I felt positive.

I knew that it probably wouldn't last, but, for the first time since leaving the havoc of France, I felt like my old self again. I felt like if I walked a few miles back in the direction I'd just come from, I could negotiate my way back in, and secure myself a few bottles of whiskey in the process.

I had hopped off the bus a mile away, deciding that walking the last little bit would do me the world of good. I stood at the crest of the hill that gently sloped downwards and into the sleepy little village. It was like there was no war here, as if a few months ago this part of the country hadn't been swarming with men, men from all over the world; Britain, America, Canada, India, the list was as long as my arm.

The idyllic scene that lay before me, the quaint, quiet English village, boxed in by dry stone walls as they marked out the surrounding fields, helped to steady my mind considerably. It was then that I decided this is where I belonged, where I would live.

The pulsations throbbed back up into my chest again as another engine came within reach of my hearing. I couldn't see it, and in a way, I found myself wishing that I couldn't, but I knew that somewhere near, another Halifax bomber was coming in to land, probably in preparation for another training mission.

It was a fantastic beast, the Halifax. Powered by four, seemingly unstoppable engines, I had spent many hours towed behind them as they took us to our target for the day. The Halifax crews would treat each sortie with the utmost severity and professionalism, but on more than one occasion we had shared hand gestures with the rear gunner while he sat, bored and alone.

RAF Tarrant Rushton was just a few miles away. It had been my home for the last two years and I had loved every minute of it. I was good at what I did and that meant that I could get away with almost anything on the base.

Acquiring things that other people require had always come naturally to me, whether it was acquiring things legally or not. Being placed on a military base made the demand for someone like me incredibly high, and consequently I had a lot of friends. On the other hand, I had made myself plenty of enemies too as I took advantage of lax security and easily persuaded quartermasters.

For the first time in ages, I found myself smirking at a happy memory, to no one in particular, as the tremor caused by the Merlin engine subsided as it began to shut down. But it was quickly replaced by a very different kind of vibration.

Tap. Tap. Tap.

My hands quivered as I released the brass door knocker after I'd given it a few short, sharp taps. The housing piece of the knocker was in the shape of a lion, its mouth gripping tightly to the handle itself. I found myself staring at it intently, as if I'd never seen something so outrageous and marvellous in my life.

The lion was replaced by a woman, a young woman. She was just as beautiful as he had told me, and more so. He always had a humbler approach to things than I did, and she was one thing that I would struggle to remain humble about.

She was smaller than I had imagined, Charlie had often told me how she came up shorter in comparison to him, but I had always thought it was his own unique way of teasing her a little bit, even if she wasn't with him to respond.

She had a kind face, the sort of face you knew that she

would be welcoming and sweet in any situation, which was good news for me, because I had just turned up on her doorstep uninvited. Despite that though, her eyes were ferocious, glinting green in the now-fading sunlight. She had a kind atmosphere about her, a calming character, but her eyes gave her away as one that could be fierce and fiery if she needed to be, used to standing up for herself against all the odds.

I could feel the warmth of the dipping sun gently kiss my neck, and the orangey hues of the fading daylight only served to highlight her beauty, as she eyed me up and down, profiling me in much the same way as I had done to her.

The qualities that I had deduced from her face had only taken me a couple of seconds of looking at her, she was captivating. I could see how Charlie had fallen for her so easily, every part of her gave something away, something more intriguing than the last.

They had met down here, in Dorset, after Charlie had pursued her after getting a glimpse of her at a local dance. He had seen her, but not for long and we left the dance soon after, making Charlie, uncharacteristically, sneak off the base to see if he would be able to track her down. In the creepiest act of romance that I had ever heard of, he had managed to find her and quite soon after, Charlie had started to wear a wedding band on his ring finger every time I saw him.

It hadn't taken very long to find her, it was a relatively small village and it turned out she was quite well known in the area, so was Charlie it seemed. The greengrocer was more than happy to point me in the direction of her house, without even asking who I was. The "Careless Talk Costs

Lives" poster and the figures looking out at the observer looked hilariously out of place in his shop.

She broke the deadlock, clearly growing impatient at the ensuing silence on her doorstep.

"John," it was a statement of fact more than an inquisitive remark, almost like she had been waiting in all day for me. A minute or two must have passed before she spoke again.

"Come in, please," she spoke softly, as if I was a child and, as she turned and shuffled down the hallway, I realised that the tone of her voice matched her face perfectly.

She busied herself making me a cup of tea before placing it on a table stationed to the left of the arm. She took a chair on the opposite side of the room, facing the fireplace. I could just about hear the wireless crackling away in what I assumed was the kitchen, and the constant ticking of the clock above the fireplace was incessant.

The scratching nib of the clock began to irritate me, and the involuntary tapping of my fingernails on the arm of the chair began in earnest. I needed to cut away from it, move my mind away from the ticking and focus on something else.

Tap. Tap. Tap.

I thought of Charlie, how would he feel knowing that I was sat in his armchair, in his home? Would he have been pleased to know that I had made an effort with his wife? Or would an intense burning of jealousy be raging up in him? I concluded that I would probably find out when I went to bed.

I sat for a while, unable to speak. How did this work? How was this woman, this stranger, going to help rid me of my nightmares and get my life back on track? This woman had been widowed, at a young age too, and here I was thinking just of my situation once more.

To me, it felt like only a few minutes had passed but the darkness of the sky told me plainly that I had been sat here for quite some time.

"I'm just going to check on the baby, I won't be a minute."

This was the third or fourth time that she had said this now, each time I responded with an even longer silence than the last. My uneasiness of the whole situation began to grow, especially after I found myself staring at a yellowing wedding veil, that was draped rather ceremoniously across the front window of the house.

She re-entered the room, this time wrapped up tightly in a dressing gown, I'd clearly outstayed my welcome. I suddenly felt intensely stupid. I had wasted my only opportunity. But only because I didn't know what to say, I hadn't thought it through at all. I had just expected her to say something, do something that meant that my head would be fixed forever. Forgiveness, maybe? A hug? I hadn't done the right thing.

Silently, I got up to leave.

"Stay?" she said, quietly at first, but she became more confident with the next, "Stay the night?"

I stood, with an obvious perplexed look on my face.

"Up the stairs, on the right, the spare room. He'd always wanted you to come and visit."

She spoke sympathetically, not entirely how I'd expected a twenty-two-year-old widow to react to this situation, especially at such a late hour as it now was.

I felt one edge of my mouth raise up slightly at the

mention of him. I didn't feel fearful of him here, he wasn't an enemy figure charging towards me, he was my friend, my brother, the one who had kept an eye out for me all the time we had been together. I felt closer to him here.

The room was bare, except for a pre-made bed and a small table beside it, upon which a miniature lamp sat proudly. It seemed as if no one had used this room before, but it was kept in a constant state of readiness for anyone who might happen to drop in.

She pulled the blackout blind over the window, as she justified to me why she didn't feel the need for a blind in here if the door was always shut. I wanted to reassure her that I wasn't going to grass her up to the Civil Defence warden any time soon, if they had one round here. But nothing would come out of my mouth.

"Do you need pyjamas?" I didn't like where this was going, the only pyjamas she would surely have in the house would be Charlie's and I didn't much like the thought of what he would have to say to me later on in my mind.

"I had to come," the words shot out of my mouth, faster than a round was ejected from a machine gun. My mouth had gone dry, which was strange as I'd had plenty of tea and water to keep me going, it ached as I had to strain to make every syllable audible to her. Even then I wasn't entirely sure she'd heard me, she just seemed to continue fiddling with the blind.

"I…I had to," I felt the words pathetically fade away into the emptiness of the bedroom.

"He's in my mind, Christine. He's there all the time, I thought coming here might help me…and him."

She remained silent as she shuffled around the room,

making herself look a lot busier than she actually was. The room was immaculate but no matter how many times she brushed the bed with the palm of her hand, another lump would require her attention.

"No, thank you," I found myself uttering, "I'll sleep in my clothes, it… it usually helps." I tried to give her a reassuring smile, but probably only achieved a weak flickering of my lips.

She left me to it. Before she shut the door completely, her head appeared through the crack, the faint ticking of the clock just about detectable from downstairs.

"I know you had to come, John. It'll do you good," and with that, she was gone.

7

6th June 1944
01.36 hours

EVERYTHING WAS in a complete silence now, the void of any noise dangled there limply, like a man who had just experienced the cruel snap of the hangman's noose. The corporal had stopped running around and half-whispering, half-screaming at us. There was no more low-level chatter accompanied by the odd chuckle or swear word in retaliation. Everything was in complete silence.

Even the tank seemed to have fallen silent for now. The tank tracks squealed to a halt, before the idling engine seemed to shut down. There was nothing, no whistle of a summertime breeze, no fluttering of a disturbed bat, as if even Mother Nature was taunting us in the silence. Only the sound of my faltering breathing shattered the stillness.

Crouching down next to me, Charlie passed me a

slimy, half-melted piece of my chocolate, which I accepted, dropping it on to my tongue before sliding it down my throat. I had always marvelled at chocolate, one of the simplest and yet most exotic of things that I had ever tasted. I dreamt of the far-flung land that the cocoa bean had come from, the hard work that had endured to turn it into the simple pleasure of sweet, glistening, half-melted chocolate.

He continued to fiddle with the wrapper for a moment, before folding it over the remaining pieces and popping it into his breast pocket.

I looked up from him as he tapped it and he gave me a wink.

"It's lucky," he mouthed.

He'd perked up. Not more than five minutes ago, I wouldn't have put it past him to jump in front of the tank and scream at it to kill him. Now, he looked more fired up than ever, like he had something to fight for.

My eardrums were almost shattered as the tank's engines fired up again, an oily, greasy smell filling the night sky as they did so. My nerves gave way as the revs increased as the pistons began to settle into their usual rhythm. I could feel them almost taunting me.

Tap. Tap. Tap.

A voice sparked up, a German voice, I was sure of it. It was closely followed by a squeal of a hinge, presumably as the hatch on the tank was closed and locked. The squeal was simultaneously joined by the shriek of tank tracks.

They were back on the move. They were coming towards us.

They knew we were here, they must have known that we weren't just going to leave the bridge to them. They can't have been as stupid and lazy as we'd been made to believe.

But still, they continued to drive nonchalantly towards the bridge, as if they were on a sightseeing tour of quaint little French villages. It was a nice village, only a few houses here and there and the canals running through it, it must have been so tranquil during the day. I had seen there was a small café on this side of the bridge, a Bren gun team now occupying it. I thought that I should return one day, sit and have a coffee or something stronger, and marvel at the serene French countryside that surrounded me. But this was 2am in the morning. And they were in a Panzer IV tank. This was definitely not a sightseeing trip.

I braced myself as the trembling of the tank's tracks began to reverberate on the ground around me, turning my legs into shivering wrecks. It was fortunate that I was lying, huddled into the wall of sandbags, rather than up on my feet or they certainly would have given way. I had lost all power in them. Like I had lost all control of everything.

I clamped my eyes shut tight and pursed my lips tighter still as I waited and prayed for the sound of a PIAT round piercing the tank and relieving us all of any duty.

But it wasn't coming. The tank kept getting closer and closer to us. I opened my eyes, Charlie's were wide with fear, like a deer who sees a man with a rifle staring straight at him. We knew it was coming, but the waiting was making the process of dying even worse.

The Projector, Infantry, Anti-Tank gun was a detestable weapon, I had hated it every time that I had trained on it, and actively stayed away from it at every possible opportunity. But here I was, crouching behind a flimsy sandbag wall, praying to hear the odd *fffwiipp* that it made as the two-and-a-half-pound bomb was limply propelled from it.

The tank rolled closer still. It would be too late now, I could chance a look without being at risk of having my head blown off, the trajectory of the gun turret would mean it couldn't aim so low.

I peeked over the top.

It was a formidable looking beast, and a well armoured one at that. It was well built, I could hardly make out any welding joints or rivets like I had been able to do on other ones that I had seen. It had a large sheet of steel that hung over the top half of the actual tracks, protecting them from any high explosives, for example, like that from a PIAT gun. Another indicator of how well prepared this army was compared to our own.

I was now fairly convinced that my fate had been sealed. There was no way a PIAT would be able to penetrate and destroy this tank. In fact, I may as well stand up and offer my capitulation right now.

I didn't, instead I sat, staring at it, partly in fear but mainly in utter admiration of the thing. It stirred up a feeling of utter jealousy within me, what I would have done to have a beast like that on our side of the bridge. The envy that built up within me made tiny beads of sweat roll through the valleys and creases on my hands, as I pictured the smug face of the officer inside, watching, waiting, to give the execution order.

Its turret was facing dead ahead, aiming perfectly out and along the bridge, it had it all covered, it was ready to pounce.

Tap. Tap. Tap.

I caught a flash of light just away to my left, and just as

I flicked my head round to take a glimpse at it, an intense heat, a burning sensation hit the right-hand side of my face, followed by a blinding flash.

I just caught the silhouette of a figure clutching onto a PIAT gun, it's distinctive rocket shape projectile noticeably absent from its frame.

Suddenly, I was thrown into a deep darkness, as my eyes came round from the sudden shockwaves of light that I had just experienced. I was blind for a moment, but within a fraction of a second, my eyesight was more or less back to normal.

There were sudden, muffled shouts from within the tank, and it rocked back briefly as it spewed out a burning hot shell. The shell exploded somewhere just to my left and behind me, but I wasn't able to see the explosion.

Instead, I felt myself being launched backwards, a sandbag clearly pinned to my chest. My arms flailed around helplessly as I desperately tried to find the solid safe haven of the ground.

I felt like a new born sparrow, attempting to take off for the first time, as if I had charged off the end of a branch, wings outstretched. The wind pummelled me as I failed to stay airborne, and I charged towards the earth.

The rush of wind was louder than any I'd ever heard before, louder than being in a glider. The air was thick, and I felt myself pushing through it forcefully, as I rapidly lost altitude.

I clattered to the floor, my right arm painfully stretched up behind my back. I gasped as I fought dramatically to re-inflate my bankrupt lungs, as if a heavy weight champion had delivered one of his finest blows to my stomach.

My helmet went flying off to my left and I watched

emotionally as it rolled around before becoming inanimate. The only piece of real protective equipment we had been issued now lay some way from me. I felt vulnerable, naked.

I continued in my struggle to breathe as I felt a crushing weight on my chest and it took me a few moments to realise that the sandbag had stayed with me, still strapped to my chest, like a baby clinging to its mother.

After a quick tussle, I managed to shift it from me and my head drooped back while I struggled for oxygen. My eyes flicked momentarily as they rolled around in my skull. I fought the urge to let them sink round and look back towards my own brain.

I coughed, spluttered and spat as I tried to rid myself of the unmistakeable, metallic twinge of blood that I found myself drowning in.

I turned my head to one side as I vomited a vibrant cocktail of blood and bile, the odd fusion of black, red and green, noticeable on my shoulder. My front teeth were now absent, and I hissed rather than breathed as my tongue obstructed my desperate panting.

The heat was intense, as if I had opened up the hatch to an immense furnace, and I struggled to keep my eyes open as I forced my head up off the floor, to take a look at the burning wreckage in front of me.

Burning silhouettes lay rolling around just a few feet from me, crying out in an undeterminable language for mercy. My eyes widened as I listened to their screams, to their cries for help.

Tap. Tap. Tap.

I focussed in on one man as I could make out a

chuckle. He began laughing almost uncontrollably, his hysterical screeching quickly turning to tears. His cries and screams were only interrupted by his necessity to briefly draw breath.

He soon began screaming, screaming so violently I could feel his vocal chords being shredded, and his howls sounded like a wounded animal that was being destroyed from the inside. His beast-like howling was the kind that the human mind cannot ignore, cannot forget.

Despite all this, I could make out a few sobs, sobs that turned into decipherable pleas.

"Chrissy…Christine…"

I could just make it out between the sobs, soon they turned to a futile effort to suck in air despite his restricted breathing.

I watched as the cacophony of intense oranges burned away in front of me, but then suddenly, everything turned to black.

8

August 1944

I WAS SOBBING AGAIN. Uncontrollably. It wasn't a dream that I'd experienced before, but I felt like I knew exactly what was going to happen next. It was a dream that had once been a reality. I had been there. I had felt and seen everything I experienced. I had remembered. I knew what came next.

I would be dragged backwards, away from the burning wreckage of the tank, its vibrant oranges lighting up the surrounding area as if a great searchlight had been focussed on it. I would witness the true callousness of the human heart as men, and bits of men, flashed past my eyes. Charlie would be dragged in to the pit alongside me a few moments later, before giving in to the intense burns that he had experienced.

The kitchen table lay on its side, the table top facing

away from me and towards the door. I sat on its underside, its legs surrounding me in a wooden bear hug. I screwed my face up and grimaced as I pushed my hands through my hair. I had felt good before, why had this new one popped up in my mind, worse than all the others?

Would they just continue on this trend for the rest of my life? I knew that if I kept seeing Charlie like that night after night, then my life wouldn't go on for much longer anyway.

"John," she said eventually, "it's alright John." Her tone was affectionate and compassionate, but I could tell that she was disturbed by the fact a near-stranger, who had invited himself into her home before screaming and crying through the night, was now a sobbing mess on the kitchen floor.

Tap. Tap. Tap.

I leapt over the table top and pressed my body hard into its surface as the *rat tat tat* of machine gun fire reverberated off the walls of the kitchen. Screaming at Christine to move I lurched out for her, dragging her into cover to wait for the racket to stop.

The Pole. Len's skull. Charlie's pleading.

She screamed as I slammed her head into the surface of the table.

The whistle of incoming mortar rounds tormented my mind, my body tensing up as I waited for the inevitable impact of the blast.

"John!" she yelled at the top of her voice, "John! Stop it now!"

Tap. Tap. Tap.

I kept her head pressed up hard against the table, my head resting on top of hers and I began breathing in individual strands of hair as my lungs began to function more normally.

My head felt as if it was splintering as I crushed my head against hers. Suddenly, I was watching from the sidelines. I watched as a man crouched down next to a dying soldier, I watched as he stared at a murdered comrade. I watched as he lay next to his pleading friend. I had no control. I could do nothing.

I watched as a sobbing wreck kept the head of a stranger pushed firmly down into a table, his own head on top of hers, both of them wincing in pain. Hers, physical, his, mental.

"John…" she managed to sneak out in between pathetic weeps and gulps for air, "it's just the kettle, John."

I rested for a moment, taking in my surroundings, taking in what she was saying to me. No sobs came from me this time, but silent tears began to splash loudly on the stone floor.

The kettle continued to squeal and rattle as it hopped from one side to the next, hollering at the nearest pair of hands to take it off the heat. It would be a few moments more before it was, a small saucer of black now situated on the bottom of it.

She sniffed as she clambered to her feet and began scuffling around again.

I rose from my position and helped her up as gently as possible, before righting the table and replacing the fallen objects. Shattered fragments of china chimed gently as my bare feet danced on it, several shards penetrating the surface of my skin, leaving small droplets dripping over the stone floor.

I blinked furiously, each one lasting longer than the

other as the burning sensation threatened to shut my eyes down for good.

"I'm sorry," I felt pathetic uttering the most futile and grovelling apology as she set about making a cup of tea. Slow, enormous waves of regret began breaking around me, and I felt as though I was lying in the surf, letting each one slowly drown me. I longed for my previous life, to take a step backwards and take a different path. What if I hadn't volunteered for gliders, would I have had a better life? Would I be normal? Would I be alive?

She scurried around almost unfazed by what had happened, as I poured out my soul to her about what had gone on. The run up to the operation, the Pole in the house, Len, Charlie and every minute detail in between. I ranted on for hours before I finally got to the end.

"….and I thought, that coming here, I might be able to say goodbye to him properly."

She left a long pause, letting me take large, sobering gulps of air as I fought against the giddiness that came down on me. I felt calmer, the haze in my mind momentarily lifted, even if the pain, hadn't yet subsided.

"He called for me?"

It wasn't the reaction that I had been expecting at all. I struggled to look at her in the eye as I thought about Charlie. I imagined the intense pain that he must have been in, the sores that had begun to form on his body almost instantly.

I tried with all my might to nod for her, but I couldn't, the weight of my tears seemed to be stopping me. She turned her back to me for a moment and took in more than her own fair share of the oxygen.

The PIAT *had* penetrated the thick armour of the tank,

it *had* done its job. But it must have hit the ammo supply inside the tank, causing an intense ball of fire and destruction, that somehow flung me backwards but engulfed Charlie.

The guilt of being alive swallowed me up once more. I had nothing to live for, I had done nothing in my life worth mentioning. I had no one to live for, but I had lived. I had lived and, yet I was wishing myself dead every minute of my waking hours.

He had called for his wife, he wanted so desperately to have her by his side, in his moment of need. He wanted to see her one, last time. I couldn't imagine how he possibly felt, I had no tangible emotions to him. I was selfish, the only person I had been thinking about was me; what was happening to me and why.

I couldn't bear the thought of thinking of someone else while I was dying, I wanted to be able to focus on myself and getting home. Maybe I was enduring this hell to teach myself something, like death was waiting for me to finally put someone else first.

I had heard him take his last breath, felt his heart beat for the last time. It was as if nature was holding him to ransom, daring him not to let his heart beat again, but he kept going, defying the calls to let go. He continued to lay there, covered in the most shattering blisters, each one searingly hot to the touch and excruciatingly painful, and yet, he was calling for his wife.

It struck me how much it seemed to mean to her that he was calling for her. I had heard of men calling for their mothers and wives before, but it was chilling that the very words that were haunting me, brought a sense of comfort and peace to her.

She had stopped cleaning the kitchen and putting things away and stood, hands on either side of the basin, staring out at some children playing on the other side of the window pane.

From what I could see, they were playing a game somewhere between hopscotch and football, a series of bobbing heads at the window, interrupted only by the occasional flash of a ball as it was lobbed at one of the bouncing scalps.

I felt a sudden urge to get up and leave, to leave and never come back, but just as I made the first movements to vacate my chair, she spoke.

"You were his best friend, John. You were all he ever spoke about. He would never tell me about what you were training to do or what he thought the ultimate goal would be. It would always be about you."

An odd sense of pride, mixed with a whole heap of awkwardness came over me and I shifted in my seat, hiding the fact that I had just tried to get up and leave.

"I know a lot about you John, I don't know whether that fills you with happiness or anxiety," she chuckled nervously.

"But you were almost like his hero."

She began to cry, and she scuttled out of the room for a moment. I sat, completely dumbfounded. How could a man like Charlie, respect someone like me? I constantly stole from stores, frequently missed training and was up on subordinate charges more than he sat on the toilet.

I heard her footsteps creak on the floorboards above my head as I continued to drown in feelings of inadequacy and total confusion.

He was from a respectable, hardworking family, and

now he was the head of his own family. He was earmarked for promotion, noted as one who would go much further than the likes of me. We were two, very different people. And yet he respected me.

I wondered if he would respect me now, sat in his kitchen with his wife, especially after I'd just brutally attacked her, all because of a kettle. Meanwhile he was condemned to an eternity of misery.

She shuffled back into the room, this time with an extra passenger on board.

"Here," she motioned for me to take the bundle of cloth in my arms, leaving me with no other option but to do as she said.

I stared down at him in utter amazement and adoration. He was perfect.

His eyes were resting but he slowly moved his limbs around in a trance like state, as only a small child can. He let out a small "coo" as he shuffled around in my arms and his innocence, the naivety of the world was beautiful. He was unblemished. He knew nothing of the evil and the suffering in the world, and I prayed on the spot that it would be a long time before he discovered what it was really like.

I raised my hand as if to stroke his face, but he stopped me. Gently, he opened his fluttering, paper thin eyelids and stared. His piercing green eyes stared back at me and he gradually moved his hand up to greet mine.

His miniature hand clamped itself over my index finger, like a bat hanging to a tree for dear life. And then, for a moment, I thought I felt something. Then again.

Was he? No, surely not.

Yes! He was! He was squeezing my finger. I almost

drowned him in great globules of tears as they splashed down around him. All the time he maintained a perfect eye contact with me, completely unblinking as the droplets crashed into his face and all around him. It was as if he knew, he knew that this is what I needed, the comfort and compassion of a small, unblemished child would help me to deal with myself, to deal with the horrors of what one man can do to another.

His innocence calmed me. It was the first time since Normandy that I had had a positive thought about another human, and for the first time, he had given me hope. Hope that a child *can* be brought into such a world as this and still maintain a perfect, untouched innocence.

"He's beautiful."

"You were his best friend John. I don't know exactly what you saw out there or what you experienced, but I know that you were always with him, and that brings great comfort to a widow." She spoke matter-of-factly, it was as if she had already got over Charlie, no emotion in her voice at all.

I shuffled once more in my seat, still clutching to the new life that was in my arms.

"You were always a part of him John, and now he'll always be a part of you.

"He's called Charlie, by the way." I looked up with a half-smile on my face. I would have done the same.

"Charlie…John."

I looked up at her, the great waterfalls that had filled up my eyes blurred my vision completely and they cascaded downwards as I looked back at the small child.

Charlie John Manning. I liked it.

PART III

1

September 1985

My Dad died nearly fifteen years ago now, and he took what he had experienced to the grave with him. Still, to this day I do not know how he made it out of that burning box alive, and now I never will. That afternoon before I went to war was the only time he had spoken to me about what had happened to him and, as far as I know, he never spoke to anyone about it ever again.

He continued to carry his scars, the visual, physical reminders of what had happened to him. But they didn't matter, there were ointments and pills that he could take that would give him some respite from the pain. It was the ones in his mind that continued to torment him, continue to taunt me, and it is those scars, that will never leave.

I never asked him if it had made him feel any better to explain, we never spoke of it ourselves after that, but it had seemed he had needed that one release, that one opportunity to pour his mind out to someone else, share the burden. This is what this is. I do not know yet if it has helped me, I do not know if it ever will, but, to an extent I feel like I have shared the burden with you. I pray every day that you will never experience what I did, I beg that you never even come close, but, if you do, you must always hold fast, and settle things as much as possible within your own mind.

Talk about it if that's what it takes. Write about it. Share the burden.

The "battle fatigue" that Major Lewis diagnosed me with, still looms over me, clings to me, even forty years on. I sleep now, the dreams have subsided, but the memories that I possess still haunt me daily.

I still walk with a limp, a small piece of shrapnel embedded in my upper thigh. There's no point in trying to remove it now, it will do more harm than good, so it will always be a part of me. It doesn't hurt, apart from the occasional twang that is so often followed by a similar twang of uncontrollable guilt.

The dreams have eased, the names have faded but the memory is still so painfully vivid. I cannot escape what I have seen, what I have done, even forty years later. People call me a hero and I let them, not because I think they're right, but because they do not understand what their heroes have actually done. Their heroes are murderers, interrogators, thieves, but most of all, they are simply damaged.

Their heroes have seen and done some of the most horrific things that one man can do to another, but yet, it was all done in the name of righteousness and freedom. A necessity of war. It's hard to think like that when you're on the battlefield. Out there, it's man versus man, not democracy versus totalitarianism. Out there, you have to kill a man to survive. One minute you are fighting a living, breathing human, one with a family and friends, with aspirations and goals, maybe even sympathies with you. The next, he is just a slab of meat, lying on the floor, a pool of blood slowly filling up around him.

No one, unless you have truly been there yourself, can ever fully understand what taking a life feels like. To be there when the eyes stop seeing and the breathing ceases forever. No one can ever understand what that felt like to me. I am selfish, I do only think of myself, but understand this, it's because of what has happened to me, I've seen things, done things that no one should ever do and seen things that no one should see. I've become self-centred, not out of a lack of compassion or sympathy for other members of this world, but out of a genuine fear of what I could do to them, even now, a sixty-something, old man.

So, my child, your grandad will never speak of the things that he has seen or done, he will just quietly mull them over and lock them away in the darkest compartment of his mind, only to let it out when he's out of sight of everyone he loves. I will never speak of it, but it is all here, my mind, laid out in ink, a physical manifestation of the memories that taunt me.

They are not here to scare you, they are not even here to warn you. They are here so that you know, so that you understand, why I am the man I am today, why I am the man who refused to wear his medals or take part in any kind of celebration of war. Maybe one day you will understand why I am the man who cries daily, watching the six o'clock news. One day.

These thoughts encompass me day after day, I never make any progress in them, they just linger, they linger there until I become too tired for the day and fall asleep. Then, I'll repeat the whole process again tomorrow.

I am not the only man who now thinks like this. It is not just the men that deal with these thoughts either. There is an entire generation of us, all of your Grandad's friends and contemporaries are scarred in one way or another. We cannot tell you what we have seen or done, we cannot identify ourselves as suffering individuals. But we are there. *We* are the man waiting at the bus stop, or the lady struggling with her change at the checkout. *We* are in the doctor's waiting room or walking down the street. We are strangers to you. Or we might even be a part of your family.

I came back, and I thank God, every day for letting me, but others didn't. I was able to return, make something of my life and build a family around me, a loving family. Soon, when you are born, I will become a grandparent, a new, tiny child will fill my attention. One that is completely oblivious to this life, to its corruptibility, the nature of humankind and its nonchalant view of life.

I don't want to be a grandparent who hides things. In my older life, I have found myself yearning for the world, willing the world to put aside its differences and come together in peace. The conclusion that I have come to is, sadly, it will never happen. But I *can* make a difference.

I am a man who has been to war, one who has killed to make things right and although we won *that* war, another one will be along soon, and the killing will start again.

I want to end these stories, one man at a time, they

need to see what war, what killing, does to a man's soul. It breaks it beyond repair.

I fulfilled my promise to myself that I'd made all those years ago when I visited Christine. I live in a leafy suburban village in the south of England. There are no planes overhead here, no unnecessary vehicles trundling around, no sirens screaming or people shouting; I am left alone with my thoughts. And so, I came home, I made something of my life, I have a wife, a son and soon, a grandson. But I will never escape. I have never escaped. I survived, but often, I find myself asking how much of me died over there, how much of me died with Charlie and how much of Charlie survives within me?

When the dreams do come to me, they are different than before, but always the same. The maze that I'm in only ends when the morning alarm sounds and the day begins. It twists and turns and the gravel beneath my feet crunches and echoes, louder and louder with each step. Then I'll see my first monument. Charlie will be there smiling to me, encouraging me on my way through, helping to find a way out. He never gets any older, he is always the same twenty-two-year-old that had, a few minutes before, been crashed face down in a bush after being ejected from the glider.

I journey on, a little further, before I see the Pole, standing there in his best dress uniform, a grin proudly on his face. It's a smile of pride, of strength and he knows exactly what he wants from me. But it is also a smile of sorrow, a small glint in his eye as the tears reflect in the dusky twilight.

"Come on," he says in a heavily accented English, "You've got this, this is yours."

He replaces the pipe that he twiddles in his hand and inserts it slowly into the side of his mouth. Uplifted, I journey on further and see Len, who's already talking before I even reach him.

"I'm from Lancashire," he says each time, and I wonder if it's my subconscious, that he did tell me where he was from and it has resurfaced at the back of my mind. Or if it was my mind, constructing a life for Len, a background of where he was from and how he grew up, in order to give him some sort of future, other than having his brains spilled out on the fifty yards or so of steel, stretching itself over a small river.

I would see them all, encouraging me on my way, spurring me on until I got to the middle. I would begin jogging as I got closer, before sprinting my way into the clearing that would open up before me.

Each time I would skid to a halt and try to turn back, only to find that the maze had closed around me. I would be alone. Every time. There was no happy ending to this maze, no sweet chirping of birds and shrieks of delight as children ran around outside, just total, deathly silence. Just me, swamped by the perimeter of the maze all around me.

The hangman's noose would hang limply from a wooden frame, swaying gently in the breeze that rustled through the maze. I would never use it, never approach it, but would just stand and stare at it until I woke. It would taunt me, beckon me in, and on more than one occasion I have been tempted. But I always keep my feet firmly planted where they are, not moving an inch.

"Bad dream?" she would always say to me, I knew I kept her up, but I didn't want to admit to her that I needed help.

How could it be a bad dream, if it would never leave me when I woke?

Charlie had died and, at times, I felt like he was the lucky one. He had seen some of the stuff that I had seen, but he would never have to *live* with it, he would always be the twenty-two-year-old, clutching my bar of chocolate and smiling broadly. He probably didn't even work out what had hit him.

I had cheated death, but I couldn't help but feel that life, had cheated me.

Every morning when I wake, I go about my daily routine, wandering downstairs to flick the kettle on, always stopping it manually before it clicks itself off. I check the clock, force of habit, but I'd taken the batteries out some time ago, the constant ticking would cause me great discomfort. My daily life is littered with oddities and habits, all of which I have picked up to prevent the "battle fatigue" that, forty years later, I still suffer from.

So, as you grow up my child, look at me, not as an enigma, a mysterious figure who once fought in a war, but as a man who deserved to die, a man who will *never* be proud of what he has done. A man who lives in pure terror at what the next dream might bring him.

As I go about my life, the same words always saunter through my mind, from the detestable Major Lewis who I had seen so many years ago;

"ALL MEN who go to war die, son. Anyone who comes back, comes back cheated."

The End.

'As If They Were My Own' - Book 3 in the 'Gliders over Normandy' series is out now on Amazon US and Amazon UK

1

AS IF THEY WERE MY OWN

THE SCREAMS of the Stukas had died away now, and my mind drifted as I wondered about their fate. I felt incredibly guilty at the thought that they had all been shot down, now lying in a burning wreckage, smouldering in the French countryside. Part of me had hoped that they hadn't been able to bail out.

I was angry with them, they had bombed us day after day, raining terror and fear down on my boys as they desperately fought for survival. I couldn't help but think that there was an incredible cowardice in those dive bombers, a faceless murderer who scurried away back into the clouds, just as quickly as they had dived out of them. It was why I had taken pot shots at them at every opportunity I had, spreading myself out on the ground, flat on my back, rifle raised to the sky, firing off round after round at the gutless crew.

It was all pointless, but then again, everything had seemed to be pointless over the last few days. We were losing. We had fought and fought hard at that, we had lost men, lost boys, who were good at what they did and now they were left to soak into the ground, to become a part of France forever. We had pushed them back at times, a far superior army being pushed back by a small force of men who didn't have enough ammunition, or heavy weapons. But it was futile. We'd push them back, but then we'd be ordered to retreat ourselves. All that fighting, all that ammunition, all those men, all so that the enemy could just march in and take what they wanted anyway.

I hated them.

The three figures in front of me charged across the forest floor, each of their footsteps cracking and crunching on leaves and twigs. Their rifles swung from side to side as I felt every stride they took, every breath they sucked in, as they desperately made their way to some cover.

I felt sick at the thought that my own progress was being hindered. I so desperately wanted to be able to sprint as hard as them, duck behind some cover and return fire. But I couldn't, the weight was far too heavy.

He grunted with every staggered footstep that we took together. He had taken a fragment of a grenade through his boot, the force of which had melted part of it away and exposed the almost near-perfect hole that now occupied the bulk of his foot. He clung to me, and I to him, in the most deranged attempt at a three-legged race ever known to man. I laughed as I thought of what we must have looked like, and I couldn't imagine that it would be taking off in any sports days anytime soon.

His grunts brought me back to reality and as another round whined as it zipped past my ear, I felt like giving up. Ahead of me, I watched the three figures as they catapulted themselves over a fallen tree. The base of the tree had been torn away from the trunk, it lay splintered and sorrowful just to the left of my boys. It had been forcibly ripped from where it had grown for hundreds of years, probably by a mortar round, or artillery shell.

"C'mon!" I grunted, directed more at my own mind, rather than my passenger. He began to whimper, a pathetic, childlike whimpering, like the kind a naughty dog would make when caught in the act of stealing.

"Shut your mouth! Keep going!" I surprised myself with my own words, I always considered myself to be mild mannered and considerate, but here I was possessed.

"Sarge! Please! I won't make it…drop me!" I ignored his pleas, he would make it, it was only a minor wound, he could still walk on it if it really came to it.

"Shut up, Harfield! That tree, there, we're nearly there!"

We couldn't have been more than fifty or sixty yards away from the tree now. A brief respite. I knew it wouldn't be good enough, we must have had an entire German company chasing us through these woods, but it would give me time to think, to mount up a few casualties on their side, and, more importantly, let me get my breath back.

Suddenly Harfield's chest seemed to explode, and the heavy weight on my shoulder abruptly got heavier, forcing me to the ground. His face hit the deck with such a force that a pile of dried leaves seemed to flick up and a small dust cloud rose up. I had sunk to my knees with the force but knew there was no point in checking for Harfield's pulse or vital signs. Even if he was alive, I wouldn't have time to pick him up again and charge for cover, they were catching up with us, and I wouldn't appreciate going home riddled with holes and covered in blood. If they would even send me home to my wife in that state anyway.

I pushed myself up and, rifle down by my side, puffed my cheeks out violently as I began surging towards the tree. My boys behind the tree began poking their heads up, I could just make out the round, khaki steel of their helmets as they did so. In a way, I was grateful that they weren't firing yet, as I began dancing left and right, zigzagging and darting as unpredictably as possible. I hoped that it would make it harder to hit me, and as I flicked behind one tree, I heard a sobering, solid *thump* as a round hammered into the bark.

Harfield was dead. That was another good bloke that I had lost, I was now up to fourteen in the space of twenty-four hours. I thought it was fourteen, it could easily have been more, they were the only ones that I'd actually seen killed with my own eyes. I'd probably lost a lot more than that now, most of them had gone their separate ways and so I had no way of protecting them at all.

I made it to the log, just as the barrels of three Lee-Enfield rifles reluctantly rested themselves on the top of the trunk. I threw myself head first over the log, diving into a pool of dried leaves and twigs. Spitting some of them out of my mouth I tried my best to gather my thoughts, to calm myself in amongst the utter chaos that seemed to be getting the better of us.

"We're lost! We're completely lost! Admit it, we're never getting home, are we?!" Vidler was one of the least liked blokes in the company. He had been a petty thief in civvie street, who had chosen military life instead of six months inside. It just so happened that his time in the army had seemingly coincided with a massive German advance through France and Belgium. It couldn't have happened to a nicer bloke.

He routinely skipped duties and on more than one occasion had been arrested by the military police for multiple bar fights and being too physical in the local 'houses of interest'. He was foul mouthed and had a lack of respect for everybody else in his company, something that was reciprocated from all the other boys.

"I've got everything to live for! This is so unfair, I don't want to be here! Why are we protecting the French anyway?! It's their problem, let them deal with it!" His rant continued, and he began to flap, every sentence becoming more hysterical than the last.

"Why didn't we just leave him?! He slowed us down so much, we'd be at the coast if it wasn't for Harfield!" His voice was dangerously loud, the Germans already knew exactly where we were, but I didn't want to advertise it any more than was strictly necessary.

It was also having a bad effect on us, because I knew he was right. We all did. It would have been more sensible to leave him when we got into trouble, to prop him up against a tree and hope that a kindly German medic would patch him up. But it wasn't the *right* thing to do, and I couldn't help but do the right thing, it was something I was susceptible to.

"You've done this to us, Baker, you!" He more or less spat his words at me, the utter contempt in his voice was on a level that I had never heard before.

Corporal Carter shuffled his way over to Vidler, creating a wash of leaves behind him as he scraped along. Delivering the finest punch square on Vidler's nose, he hissed at him, "It's Sergeant Baker, Vidler. And the only reason we're still 'ere is because of 'im."

I smirked at him, something that he took as a sign of thanks, and he shuffled back to his position, picking up his rifle on the way.

Vidler sobbed quietly as he mopped up the blood on the sleeve of his wool jacket. It had already begun to drip down and form up on the collar of his jacket as he spat out a mouthful of blood-stained saliva onto the ground.

"You pull yourself together," I said, not looking at him, "and make sure you do it quick."

A subdued "Sarge…" uttered from his lips, half-heartedly, but it didn't matter, all I needed was to make sure that he would fire his weapon at the right time, and at the right people.

As I looked out across the wood, all seemed totally quiet for a moment. There was no more shouting, no more bullets zipping over our heads, even the faint booming of artillery had seemed to fall silent, all for us.

GET A FREE BOOK TODAY

YOU CAN HELP MAKE A DIFFERENCE

Reviews are one of my most powerful weapons in generating attention for my books.
Unfortunately, I do not have a blockbuster budget when it comes to advertising but
Thanks to you I have something better than that.

Honest reviews of my books helps to grab the attention of other readers so, even if you have one minute, I would be incredibly grateful if you could leave me a review on whichever Amazon store suits you.

THANK YOU SO MUCH.

ABOUT THE AUTHOR

Thomas Wood is the author of the 'Gliders over Normandy' book series, as well as the upcoming series surrounding Lieutenant Alfie Lewis, a young Royal Tank Regiment officer in 1940s France.

He posts regular updates on his website www.ThomasWoodBooks.com

and is also contactable by email at ThomasWoodBooks@outlook.com

Printed by Amazon Italia Logistica S.r.l.
Torrazza Piemonte (TO), Italy

16231749R00125